THE STRANGE &
MYSTERIOUS TALES
OF
F. SCOTT FITZGERALD

INCLUDING
THE CURIOUS CASE OF
BENJAMIN BUTTON

Read & Co.

Copyright © 2022 Fantasy & Horror Classics

This edition is published by Fantasy & Horror Classics,
an imprint of Read & Co.

British Library Cataloguing-in-Publication Data
A catalogue record for this book is available
from the British Library.

Read & Co. is part of Read Books Ltd.
For more information visit
www.readandcobooks.co.uk

CONTENTS

F. Scott Fitzgerald

F. Scott Fitzgerald was born on 24th September 1896 in Saint Paul, Minnesota, USA.

Born to an upper-middle-class family, Fitzgerald was named after his famous lawyer second cousin, Francis Scott Key, But was referred to as Scott. His early education was at two Catholic schools in Buffalo, New York, first the Angels Convent, where he attended lessons for only half of the school day (he was allowed to choose which half) and then Nardin Academy. At an early age he was recognised as being of unusual intelligence and developed a keen interest in literature.

In 1908, his family returned to Minnesota due to his father being fired from Proctor & Gamble. While in Minnesota he attended St. Paul Academy and began his career as a fiction writer, having his first story printed in the school newspaper at the age of 13. He then moved to a prestigious Catholic prep school, Newman School in Jersey, before graduating in 1913 and enrolling at Princeton University.

He became immersed in the literary culture at Princeton, making friends with future writers and critics such as John Peale Bishop and Edmund Wilson, and writing for university publications including *The Princeton Tiger* and the *Nassau Lit.* His studies, however, suffered due to his literary pursuits and in 1917 he dropped out of education to join the U.S. Army and fight in World War I. He had made a couple of submissions of novels to publisher Charles Scribner's Sons but both were rejected even though his writing style was praised. One of these was *The Romantic Egoist,* hastily written before reporting for military duty for fear that he may die in the ensuing fighting. This novel was later revised and accepted in 1919 under the title *This Side of Paradise.*

While serving as a second lieutenant in Montgomery, Alabama, Fitzgerald met his future wife, Zelda Sayre, daughter of an Alabama Supreme Court justice. When the war ended in 1918, he and Zelda wedded, and in 1921 had their first and only child, Frances Scott "Scottie" Fitzgerald.

During the 1920's *Jazz Age* Fitzgerald became enchanted with the expatriate community in Paris, visiting several times and making influential friends such as Ernest Hemingway. He continued his career writing short stories for magazines such as 'The Saturday Evening Post', Collier's Weekly', and Esquire, whilst at the same time perusing his ambitions as a novelist.

He and Zelda lived an opulent lifestyle as New York celebrities, but all was not roses. Fitzgerald was well known as a heavy drinker and struggled with financial difficulties. He was constantly borrowing money from his literary agent, Harold Ober, but when Ober decided to cut him off, Fitzgerald severed ties with his long-time friend. These financial problems became even more worrisome when Zelda was diagnosed as having schizophrenia in 1930. She was hospitalised and remained fragile for the rest of her life. This inspired his final complete novel *Tender is the Night* (1934), which tells the story of a young psychoanalyst, Dick Diver, and his wife, Nicole, who is also one of his patients.

In 1937 Fitzgerald moved to Hollywood where he continued writing short stories and working on projects for the film company Metro-Goldwyn-Mayer. While there, Fitzgerald he began a relationship with gossip columnist Sheilah Graham, with whom he lived whilst, now estranged, Zelda remained in mental institutions on the East Coast.

His alcoholism had been a part of his life since college, but by the late 1930's it began to seriously impact his health. It was his third heart attack that killed him and he was pronounced dead on 21st December 1940, aged just 44.

He is remembered as one of the greatest American writers of the 20th Century. His work, *The Great Gatsby* (1925), though not highly praised during his life-time, is considered to be his magnum opus and is often on reading lists of English literature students around the world.

THE JAZZ AGE
LITERATURE OF THE
LOST GENERATION

An Introductory Essay

The Jazz Age is one of the most significant cultural movements in American history. Coinciding with the Roaring Twenties, the Prohibition Era, and women being granted the right to vote, the era that spanned from the First World War up to the Wall Street Crash in 1929 was a period of considerable social reform. The war had displaced thousands of Americans, with people not only losing loved ones but also their sense of purpose and direction in life. With a generation reeling from such devastation, life following the war was one of optimism, full of hope and determination for a better future. It allowed the young people to rebel against the traditional ideals that came before, exploring new artistic endeavours that helped shape a new glittering and prosperous society. Eventually becoming known as the Lost Generation, it was this wave of young people who helped form the Jazz Age of 1920s post-war America.

While the period of The Lost Generation is commonly known as America's liberating Jazz Age, jazz music had been around for many decades before then. The swinging genre of jazz began in New Orleans, Louisiana, in the late nineteenth century, with its roots in ragtime and blues. The expressive, rhythmic music originated in the pain and oppression of slavery in the United States. Black-American communities popularised the music in the early 1920s during the prohibition of alcohol. It was popular in illegal speakeasies and became a widespread genre with the rise of radio, rebelling against the traditional, popular music of the time. Jazz came to represent a sense of freedom for the people of a country devastated by oppression, war, and loss, and formed the soundtrack for the hedonistic culture of the Roaring Twenties.

Despite the era's culture being grounded in music, many prolific literary figures belonged to the Lost Generation, including the likes of F. Scott Fitzgerald and Ernest Hemingway. A term first coined by American writer Gertrude Stein and popularised by Hemingway in his 1926 novel, *The Sun Also Rises*, the definition of the Lost Generation applies to those born between 1883 and 1900 who came of age during World War I. The pioneering modernist work produced by authors during this period popularised an entirely new literary style and sensibility, championing the indulgent lifestyle the era became synonymous with.

As America moved away from its post-war sorrow, the country entered into a period of ecstasy and celebration. Technology was developing faster than ever, and America's economy rapidly expanded. The illegal trafficking of alcohol, known as bootlegging, was at its height, and speakeasies were immensely popular. As the economy grew, people became more frivolous and extravagant in spending. Cocktails and dances such as the Charleston were all the rage, and with the 19th Amendment granting women the right to vote, young people had newfound freedom. Jazz culture instigated a substantial societal shift. People of all races, genders, and backgrounds were mixing in underground bars. The decade gave way to new forms of self-expression and youth culture. It was the age of flapper girls, materialism, excessive drinking, and artistic genius.

The new social frivolity was captured in the decade's literature. Despite the term 'Jazz Age' being in existence before his writings, it was F. Scott Fitzgerald who popularised the phrase with the publication of his second collection of short stories, *Tales of the Jazz Age* (1922). One of the most influential writers of the Lost Generation, Fitzgerald's masterful works, including the now famous novel *The Great Gatsby* (1925), perfectly encapsulates the spirit of the time.

In the aftermath of the war, many members of the Lost Generation felt the US no longer had anything to offer them, so they took to travelling. Europe called to the artists who were seeking escape from the rising commercialism in the States, and it was in Paris that the likes of Hemingway and Fitzgerald first found their footing as authors, rubbing shoulders with the literary elite in the Parisian salons and cafés.

Often regarded as the mother of the Lost Generation writers, Gertrude Stein formed her own literary salon in Paris where poets, authors, musicians, and artists were able to seek guidance and counsel among peers. Similarly, Shakespeare and Company, an English-language lending library and bookstore in Paris, was also a haven for authors. American publisher Sylvia Beach opened the store in November 1919, with Stein signing up as her first annual subscriber. It's said that the store often served as a makeshift bedroom for Fitzgerald and Hemingway, amongst other writers.

Stein's memoir spoof, *The Autobiography of Alice B. Toklas* (1933), describes many of her encounters with the Lost Generation writers from the perspective of her life partner, Alice B. Toklas. The book is an account of the couple's time living in Paris during the Jazz Age, giving insight into the pair's relationship with these influential literary figures. From the likes of Sylvia Beach and Ezra Pound to T. S. Eliot and Carl Van Vechten, Stein and Toklas formed many literary friendships and connections in Paris, even becoming Godparents to Hemingway's first child.

While the era was a time of prosperity and hope, the war had caused long-lasting effects on the generations that followed. Young people were entering the 1920s with war wounds, both physical and emotional. Writers started to find escape within their art, creating written accounts of their experiences with the war becoming a common theme of Jazz Age literature. William Faulkner's first novel, *Soldiers' Pay* (1926), examines the reality of many returning soldiers. It explores the post-war life of a severely wounded aviator after he returns home and discovers he no longer has a purpose in his small town. Similar in its post-war themes, Hemingway's debut novel, *The Sun Also Rises* (1926), follows protagonist Jake Barnes as he navigates life after war. Based on Hemingway himself the main character is recovering from war wounds whilst working as a journalist in Paris. The early novel dismisses Stein's 'lost generation' label and proposes that they are not 'lost' but merely downtrodden by war. Exploring issues of artistic freedom, gender, love, and angst, *The Sun Also Rises* captures the essence of the disoriented generation.

Despite the existentialist questions that many of the Lost Generation writers addressed in their work, the Jazz Age also saw a significant shift in artists' sense of freedom. Writers were beginning to test the limits of literature, and modernist experimentation heightened. One of the most experimental writers of this time was e. e. cummings, whose work is rich in his war experiences. While serving as an ambulance driver in the war, cummings was arrested and imprisoned by the French on suspicion of espionage. This experience later informed the writing of his only novel, *The Enormous Room* (1922), which not only explores the psychological impact of war but also demonstrates his blossoming avant-garde writing style. The collections of poetry that followed, including *Tulips and Chimneys* (1923), *XLI Poems* (1925), & (1926), and *is 5* (1926), ignore traditional form and grammar rules, experiment with typographical presentation, and focus on taboo themes such as eroticism through an aggressive rebellion of accepted literary norms.

The Jazz Age not only gave the Lost Generation artistic freedom but also freedom of speech. Women now had the right to vote and could express themselves more independently.

Through their newfound freedom, it became common for women to wear their hair short, dress in tight clothing, and smoke in public—a stereotype character consistently filling the pages of literature at the time. Anita Loos' comic novel *Gentlemen Prefer Blondes* (1925) is a prime example of this. The book features Lorelei Lee, a young blonde flapper, following her gold-digging escapades and numerous romantic flings around the world. Presented as Lorelei's diary, *Gentlemen Prefer Blondes* is full of Loos' famous wisecracks and takes the reader across the globe from New York and Paris to London and Munich, giving an insightful look at the Jazz Age on the way.

Another novel, *Firecrackers* (1925) by Carl Van Vechten, also encapsulates the sense of this newfound freedom. The book is known for its audacious events and pleasure-seeking characters, with Fitzgerald labelling one of its main characters, Campaspe Lorillard, as the 'embodiment of New York'. Likewise, Fitzgerald's own novel *The Great Gatsby* encompasses the excessive drinking and spending that was a crucial part of the Lost Generation's Jazz Age experience. Set on Long Island, New York, *Gatsby* features the confusing romance, corrupt morals, and glamorous partying of the city's most wealthy socialites. The effects of the prohibition and the popularity of jazz music are as evident in Vechten's work as they are in Fitzgerald's masterpiece.

Despite being labelled as 'lost', the young generation of the Jazz Age was hopeful and driven, transforming sorrow and grief into glittering inspiration for their work. Literature greatly benefited from writers' desire to escape, both in their travel to locations such as Paris and within their work. As the economy boomed, consumerism grew, and women slowly gained independence, artists captured the extravagance of the Roaring Twenties at its peak. The Jazz Age was an era of social reform that altered post-war America tremendously; it produced many brilliant authors whose written masterpieces shaped the foundation of literature as we now know it. From Gatsby to

Hemingway, the Lost Generation writers of the American Jazz Age were driven by the lingering pain of the First World War to create works that are beautifully timeless. Embracing the chaos of post-war America to shape an era of cultural prosperity, one steeped in sparkling, glamorous indulgence.

THE MYSTERY OF
RAYMOND MORTGAGE

First Published in
Now and Then, October, 1909.

I

WHEN I first saw John Syrel of the New York Daily News, he was standing before an open window of my house gazing out on the city. It was about six o'clock and the lights were just going on. All down 33rd Street was a long line of gayly illuminated buildings. He was not a tall man, But thanks to the erectness of his posture, and the suppleness of his movement, it would take no athlete to tell that he was of fine build. He was twenty-three years old when I first saw him, and was already a reporter on the News. He was not a handsome man; his face was clean-shaven, and his chin showed him to be of strong character. His eyes and hair were brown.

As I entered the room he turned around slowly and addressed me in a slow, drawling tone: "I think I have the honor of speaking to Mr. Egan, chief of police." I assented, and he went on: "My name is John Syrel and my business,—to tell you frankly, is to learn all I can about that case of the Raymond mortgage."

I started to speak but he silenced me with a wave of his hand.

"Though I belong to the staff of the Daily News," he continued, "I am not here as an agent of the paper."

"I am not here," I interrupted coldly, "to tell every newspaper reporter or adventurer about private affairs. James, show this man out." Syrel turned without a word and I heard his steps echo up the driveway.

However, this was not destined to be the last time I ever saw Syrel, as events will show.

II

The morning after I first saw John Syrel, I proceeded to the scene of the crime to which he had alluded. On the train I picked up a newspaper and read the following account of the crime and theft, which had followed it:

EXTRA
GREAT CRIME COMMITTED IN SUBURBS OF
CITY MAYOR PROCEEDING TO SCENES OF CRIME

On the morning of July 1st, a crime and serious theft were committed on the outskirts of the city. Miss Raymond was killed and the body of a servant was found outside of the house. Mr. Raymond of Santuka Lake was awakened on Tuesday morning by a scream and two revolver shots which proceeded from his wife's room. He tried to open the door but it would not open. He was almost certain the door was locked from the inside, when suddenly it swung open disclosing a room in frightful disorder. On the center of the floor was a revolver and on his wife's bed was a bloodstain in the shape of a hand. His wife was missing, but on a closer search he found his daughter under the bed, stone dead. The window was broken in two places. Miss Raymond had a bullet wound on her body and her head was fearfully cut. The body of a servant was found outside with a bullet hole through his head. Mrs. Raymond has not been found. The room was upset. The bureau drawers were out as if the murderer had been looking for something. Chief of Police Egan is on the scene of the crime, etc., etc.

Just then the conductor called out "Santuka!" The train came to a stop, and getting out of the car I walked up to the house. On the porch I met Gregson, who was supposed to be the ablest detective in the force. He gave me a plan of the house which he said he would like to have me look at before we went in.

"The body of the servant," he said, "is that of John Standish. He has been with the family 12 years and was a perfectly honest man. He was only 32 years old."

"The bullet which killed him was not found?" I asked.

"No," he answered; and then, "Well, you had better come in and see for yourself. By the way, there was a fellow hanging around here, who was trying to see the body. When I refused to let him in, he went around to where the servant was shot and I saw him go down on his knees on the grass and begin to search. A few minutes later he stood up and leaned against a tree. Then he came up to the house and asked to see the body again. I said he could if he would go away afterwards. He assented, and when he got inside the room he went down on his knees and under the bed and hunted around. Then he went over to the window and examined the broken pane carefully. After that he declared himself satisfied and went down towards the hotel."

After I had examined the room to my satisfaction, I found that I might as well try to see through a millstone as to try to fathom this mystery. As I finished my investigation I met Gregson in the laboratory.

"I suppose you heard about the mortgage," said he, as we went down stairs. I answered in the negative, and he told me that a valuable mortgage had disappeared from the room in which Miss Raymond was killed. The night before Mr. Raymond had placed the mortgage in a drawer and it had disappeared.

On my way to town that night I met Syrel again, and he bowed cordially to me. I began to feel ashamed of myself for sending him out of my house. As I went into the car the only vacant seat was next to him. I sat down and apologized for my rudeness of the day before. He took it lightly and, there being nothing to say, we sat in silence. At last I ventured a remark.

"What do you think of the case?"

"I don't think anything of it as yet. I haven't had time yet."

Nothing daunted I began again. "Did you learn anything?"

Syrel dug his hand into his pocket and produced a bullet. I examined it.

"Where did you find it?" I asked.

"In the yard," he answered briefly.

At this I again relapsed into my seat. When we reached the city, night was coming on. My first day's investigation was not very successful.

III

My next day's investigation was no more successful than the first. My friend Syrel was not at home. The maid came into Mr. Raymond's room while I was there and gave notice that she was going to leave. "Mr. Raymond," she said, "there was queer noises outside my window last night. I'd like to stay, sir, but it grates on my nerves."

Beyond this nothing happened, and I came home worn out.

IV

On the morning of the next day I was awakened by the maid who had a telegram in her hand. I opened it and found it was from Gregson. "Come at once," it said "startling development."

I dressed hurriedly and took the first car to Santuka. When I reached the Santuka station, Gregson was waiting for me in a runabout. As soon as I got into the carriage Gregson told me what had happened.

"Some one was in the house last night. You know Mr. Raymond asked me to sleep there. Well, to continue, last night, about one, I began to be very thirsty. I went into the hall to get a drink from the faucet there, and as I was passing from my room (I sleep in Miss Raymond's room) into the hall I heard somebody in Mrs. Raymond's room. Wondering why Mr. Raymond was up at that time of night I went into the sitting room to investigate. I opened the door of Mrs. Raymond's room. The body of Miss Raymond was lying on the sofa. A man was kneeling beside it. His face was away from me, but I could tell by his figure that he was not Mr. Raymond. As I looked he got up softly and I saw him open a bureau. He took something out and put it into his pocket. As he turned around he saw me, and I saw that he was a young man. With a cry of rage he sprang at me, and having no weapon I retreated. He snatched up a heavy Indian club and swung it over my head. I gave a cry which must have alarmed the house, for I know nothing more till I saw Mr. Raymond bending over me."

"How did this man look," I asked. "Would you know him if you saw him again?"

"I think not," he answered, "I only saw his profile."

"The only explanation I can give is this," said I. "The murderer was in Miss Raymond's room and when she came in he overpowered her and inflicted the gash. He then made for Mrs. Raymond's room and carried her off after having first shot Miss Raymond, who attempted to rise. Outside the house he met Standish, who attempted to stop him and was shot."

Gregson smiled. "That solution is impossible," he said.

As we reached the house I saw John Syrel, who beckoned me aside. "If you come with me," he said. "you will learn something that may be valuable to you."

I excused myself to Gregson and followed Syrel. As we reached the walk he began to talk.

"Let us suppose that the murderer or murderess escaped from the house. Where would they go? Naturally they wanted to get away. Where did they go? Now, there are two railroad stations near by, Santuka and Lidgeville. I have ascertained that they did not go by Santuka. So did Gregson. I supposed, therefore, that they went by Lidgeville. Gregson didn't; that's the difference. A straight line is the shortest distance between two points. I followed a straight line between here and Lidgeville. At first there was nothing. About two miles farther on I saw some footprints in a marshy hollow. They consisted of three footprints. I took an impression. Here it is. You see this one is a woman's. I have compared it with one of Mrs. Raymond's boots. They are identical. The others are mates. They belong to a man. I compared the bullet I found, where Standish was killed, with one of the remaining cartridges in the revolver that was found in Mrs. Raymond's room. They were mates. Only one shot had been fired and as I had found one bullet, I concluded that either Mrs. or Miss Raymond had fired the shot. I preferred to think Mrs. Raymond fired it because she had fled. Summing these things up and also taking into consideration that Mrs. Raymond must have had some cause to try to kill Standish, I concluded that John Standish killed Miss Raymond through the window of her mother's room, Friday night. I also conclude Mrs. Raymond, after ascertaining that her daughter was dead, shot Standish through the window and killed him. Horrified at what she had done she hid behind the door when Mr. Raymond came in. Then she ran down the back stairs. Going outside she stumbled upon the revolver Standish had used and picking it up took it with her. Somewhere between here and Lidgeville she met the owner of these footprints, either by accident or design and walked with him to the station where they took the early train for Chicago. The station master did not see the man. He says that only a woman bought a ticket, so I concluded that the young man didn't go. Now you must tell me what Gregson told you."

"How did you know all this," exclaimed I, astonished. And then I told him about the midnight visitor. He did not appear to be much astonished, and he said "I guess that the young man is our friend of the footprints. Now you had better go get a brace of revolvers and pack your suitcase if you wish to go with me to find this young man and Mrs. Raymond, whom I think is with him."

V

Greatly surprised at what I had heard I took the first train back to town. I bought a pair of fine Colt revolvers, a dark lantern, and two changes of clothing. We went over to Lidgeville and found that a young man had left on the six o'clock train for Ithaca. On reaching Ithaca we found that he had changed trains and was now half way to Princeton, New Jersey. It was five o'clock, but we took a fast train and expected to overtake him half way between Ithaca and Princeton. What was our chagrin when on reaching the slow train, to find he had gotten off at Indianous and was now probably safe. Thoroughly disappointed we took the train for Indianous. The ticket seller said that a young man in a light gray suit had taken a bus to the Raswell Hotel. We found the bus which the station master said he had taken, in the street. We went up to the driver and he admitted that he had started for the Raswell Hotel in his cab.

"But," said the old fellow, "when I reached there, the fellow had clean disappeared, an' I never got his fare."

Syrel groaned; it was plain that we had lost the young man. We took the next train for New York and telegraphed to Mr. Raymond that we would be down Monday. Sunday night, however, I was called to the phone and recognized Syrel's voice. He directed me to come at once to five hundred thirty-four Chestnut Street. I met him on the doorstep.

"What have you heard?" I asked.

"I have an agent in Indianous," he replied, "in the shape of an Arab boy whom I employ for 10 cents a day. I told him to spot the woman and today I got a telegram from him (I left him money to send one), saying to come at once. So come on." We took the train for Indianous. "Smidy," the young Arab, met us at the station.

"You see, sur, it's dis way. You says, 'Spot de guy wid dat hack,' and I says I would. Dat night a young dude comes out of er house on Pine Street and give the cabman a $10 bill. An den he went back into the house and a minute after he comes out wid a woman, an' den day went down here a little way an' goes into a house farther down the street, I'll show you de place."

We followed Smidy down the street until we arrived at a corner house. The ground floor was occupied by a cigar store, but the second floor was evidently for rent. As we stood there a face appeared at the window and, seeing us, hastily retreated. Syrel pulled a picture from his pocket. "It's she," he exclaimed, and calling us to follow he dashed into a little side door. We heard voices upstairs, a shuffle of feet and a noise as if a door had been shut.

"Up the stairs," shouted Syrel, and we followed him, taking two steps at a bound. As we reached the top landing we were met by a young man.

"What right have you to enter this house?" he demanded.

"The right of the law," replied Syrel.

"I didn't do it," broke out the young man. "It was this way. Agnes Raymond loved me--she did not love Standish--he shot her; and God did not let her murder go unrevenged. It was well

Mrs. Raymond killed him, for his blood would have been on my hands. I went back to see Agnes before she was buried. A man came in. I knocked him down. I didn't know until a moment ago that Mrs. Raymond had killed him.

"I forgot Mrs. Raymond" screamed Syrel, "where is she?"

"She is out of your power forever," said the young man.

Syrel brushed past him and, with Smidy and I following, burst open the door of the room at the head of the stairs. We rushed in.

On the floor lay a woman, and as soon as I touched her heart I knew she was beyond the doctor's skill.

"She has taken poison," I said. Syrel looked around, the young man had gone. And we stood there aghast in the presence of death.

THE ORDEAL

First published in
Nassau Literary Magazine, June, 1915

I

The hot four o'clock sun beat down familiarly upon the wide stretch of Maryland country, burning up the long valleys, powdering the winding road into fine dust and glaring on the ugly slated roof of the monastery. Into the gardens it poured hot, dry, lazy, bringing with it, perhaps, some quiet feeling of content, unromantic and cheerful. The walls, the trees, the sanded walks, seemed to radiate back into the fair cloudless sky the sweltering late summer heat and yet they laughed and baked happily. The hour brought some odd sensation of comfort to the farmer in a nearby field, drying his brow for a moment by his thirsty horse, and to the lay-brother opening boxes behind the monastery kitchen.

The man walked up and down on the bank above the creek. He had been walking for half an hour. The lay-brother looked at him quizzically as he passed and murmured an invocation. It was always hard, this hour before taking first vows. Eighteen years before one, the world just behind. The lay-brother had seen many in this same situation, some white and nervous, some grim and determined, some despairing. Then, when the bell tolled five, there were the vows and usually the novice felt better. It was this hour in the country when the world seemed gloriously apparent and the monastery vaguely impotent. The lay-brother shook his head in sympathy and passed on.

The man's eyes were bent upon his prayer-book. He was very young, twenty at the most, and his dark hair in disorder gave him an even more boyish expression. A light flush lay on his calm face and his lips moved incessantly. He was not nervous. It seemed to him as if he had always known he was to become a priest. Two years before, he had felt the vague stirring, the transcendent sense of seeing heaven in everything, that warned him softly, kindly that the spring of his life was coming. He had given himself every opportunity to resist. He had gone a year to college, four months abroad, and both experiences only increased within him the knowledge of his destiny. There was little hesitation. He had at first feared self-committal with a thousand nameless terrors. He thought he loved the world. Panicky, he struggled, but surer and surer he felt that the last word had been said. He had his vocation— and then, because he was no coward, he decided to become a priest.

Through the long month of his probation he alternated between deep, almost delirious, joy and the same vague terror at his own love of life and his realization of all he sacrificed. As a favorite child he had been reared in pride and confidence in his ability, in faith in his destiny. Careers were open to him, pleasure, travel, the law, the diplomatic service. When, three months before, he had walked into the library at home and told his father that he was going to become a Jesuit priest, there was a family scene and letters on all sides from friends and relatives. They told him he was ruining a promising young life because of a sentimental notion of self sacrifice, a boyish dream. For a month he listened to the bitter melodrama of the commonplace, finding his only rest in prayer, knowing his salvation and trusting in it. After all, his worst battle had been with himself. He grieved at his father's disappointment and his mother's tears, but he knew that time would set them right.

And now in half an hour he would take the vows which pledged him forever to a life of service. Eighteen years of study—

eighteen years where his every thought, every idea would be dictated to him, where his individuality, his physical ego would be effaced and he would come forth strong and firm to work and work and work. He felt strangely calm, happier in fact than he had been for days and months. Something in the fierce, pulsing heat of the sun likened itself to his own heart, strong in its decision, virile and doing its own share in the work, the greatest work. He was elated that he had been chosen, he from so many unquestionably singled out, unceasingly called for. And he had answered.

The words of the prayers seemed to run like a stream into his thoughts, lifting him up peacefully, serenely; and a smile lingered around his eyes. Everything seemed so easy; surely all life was a prayer. Up and down he walked. Then of a sudden something happened. Afterwards he could never describe it except by saying that some undercurrent had crept into his prayer, something unsought, alien. He read on for a moment and then it seemed to take the form of music. He raised his eyes with a start—far down the dusty road a group of negro hands were walking along singing, and the song was an old song that he knew:

> "We hope ter meet you in heavan whar we'll
> Part no mo',
> Whar we'll part no mo'.
> Gawd a'moughty bless you twel we
> Me-et agin."

Something flashed into his mind that had not been there before. He felt a sort of resentment toward those who had burst in upon him at this time, not because they were simple and primitive, but because they had vaguely disturbed him. That song was old in his life. His nurse had hummed it through the dreamy days of his childhood. Often in the hot summer afternoons he had played it softly on his banjo. It reminded him of so many things: months at the seashore on the hot beach with the gloomy ocean rolling around him, playing with sand castles with his cousin; summer evenings on the big lawn at home when he chased fireflys and the breeze carried the tune over the night to him from the negro-quarters. Later, with new words, it had served as a serenade—and now-well, he had done with that part of life, and yet he seemed to see a girl with kind eyes, old in a great sorrow, waiting, ever waiting. He seemed to hear voices calling, children's voices. Then around him swirled the city, busy with the hum of men; and there was a family that would never be, beckoning him.

Other music ran now as undercurrent to his thoughts: wild, incoherent music, illusive and wailing, like the shriek of a hundred violins, yet clear and chord-like. Art, beauty, love and life passed in a panorama before him, exotic with the hot perfumes of world-passion. He saw struggles and wars, banners waving somewhere, voices giving hail to a king—and looking at him through it all were the sweet sad eyes of the girl who was now a woman.

Again the music changed; the air was low and sad. He seemed to front a howling crowd who accused him. The smoke rose again around the body of John Wycliffe, a monk knelt at a prie-dieu and laughed because the poor had not bread, Alexander VI pressed once more the poisoned ring into his brother's hand, and the black robed figures of the inquisition scowled and whispered. Three great men said there was no God, a million voices seemed to cry, "Why! Why! must we believe?" Then as in a chrystal he seemed to hear Huxley, Nietzsche, Zola, Kant cry, "I will not"—He saw Voltaire and Shaw wild with cold passion. The voices pleaded "Why?" and the girl's sad eyes gazed at him with infinite longing.

He was in a void above the world—the ensemble, everything called him now. He could not pray. Over and over again he said senselessly, meaninglessly, "God have mercy, God have mercy." For a minute, an eternity, he trembled in the void and then—

something snapped. They were still there, but the girl's eyes were all wrong, the lines around her mouth were cold and chiselled and her passion seemed dead and earthy.

He prayed, and gradually the cloud grew clearer, the images appeared vague and shadowy. His heart seemed to stop for an instant and then—he was standing by the bank and a bell was tolling five. The reverend superior came down the steps and toward him.

"It is time to go in." The man turned instantly.

"Yes, Father, I am coming."

II

The novices filed silently into the chapel and knelt in prayer. The blessed Sacrament in the gleaming monstrance was exposed among the flaming candles on the altar. The air was rich and heavy with incense. The man knelt with the others. A first chord of the magnificat, sung by the concealed choir above, startled him; he looked up. The late afternoon sun shone through the stained glass window of St. Francis Xavier on his left and fell in red tracery on the cassock of the man in front of him. Three ordained priests knelt on the altar. Above them a huge candle burned. He watched it abstractedly. To the right of him a novice was telling his beads with trembling fingers. The man looked at him. He was about twenty-six with fair hair and green-grey eyes that darted nervously around the chapel. They caught each other's eye and the elder glanced quickly at the altar candle as if to draw attention to it. The man followed his eye and as he looked he felt his scalp creep and tingle. The same unsummoned instinct filled him that had frightened him half an hour ago on the bank. His breath came quicker. How hot the chapel was. It was too hot; and the candle was wrong—wrong—everything suddenly blurred. The man on his left caught him.

"Hold up," he whispered, "they'll postpone you. Are you

better? Can you go through with it?"

He nodded vaguely and turned to the candle. Yes, there was no mistake. Something was there, something played in the tiny flame, curled in the minute wreath of smoke. Some evil presence was in the chapel, on the very altar of God. He felt a chill creeping over him, though he knew the room was warm. His soul seemed paralyzed, but he kept his eyes riveted on the candle. He knew that he must watch it. There was no one else to do it. He must not take his eyes from it. The line of novices rose and he mechanically reached his feet.

"*Per omnia saecula, saeculorum.* Amen."

Then he felt suddenly that something corporeal was missing—his last earthly support. He realized what it was. The man on his left had gone out overwrought and shaken. Then it began. Something before had attacked the roots of his faith; had matched his world-sense against his God-sense, had brought, he had thought, every power to bear against him; but this was different. Nothing was denied, nothing was offered. It could best be described by saying that a great weight seemed to press down upon his innermost soul, a weight that had no essence, mental or physical. A whole spiritual realm evil in its every expression engulfed him. He could not think, he could not pray. As in a dream he heard the voices of the men beside him singing, but they were far away, farther away from him than anything had ever been before. He existed on a plane where there was no prayer, no grace; where he realized only that the forces around him were of hell and where the single candle contained the essence of evil. He felt himself alone pitted against an infinity of temptation. He could bring no parallel to it in his own experience or any other. One fact he knew: one man had succumbed to this weight and he must not—must not. He must look at the candle and look and look until the power that filled it and forced him into this plane died forever for him. It was now or not at all.

He seemed to have no body and even what he had thought was his innermost self was dead. It was something deeper that was he, something that he had never felt before. Then the forces gathered for one final attack. The way that the other novice had taken was open to him. He drew his breath quickly and waited and then the shock came. The eternity and infinity of all good seemed crushed, washed away in an eternity and infinity of evil. He seemed carried helplessly along, tossed this way and that—as in a black limitless ocean where there is no light and the waves grow larger and larger and the sky darker and darker. The waves were dashing him toward a chasm, a maelstrom everlastingly evil, and blindly, unseeingly, desperately he looked at the candle, looked at the flame which seemed like the one black star in the sky of despair. Then suddenly he became aware of a new presence. It seemed to come from the left, seemed consummated and expressed in warm, red tracery somewhere. Then he knew. It was the stained window of St. Francis Xavier. He gripped at it spiritually, clung to it and with aching heart called silently for God.

"Tantum ergo Sacramentum
Veneremur cernui."

The words of the hymn gathered strength like a triumphant paean of glory, the incense filled his brain, his very soul, a gate clanged somewhere and *the candle on the altar went out.*

"Ego vos absolvo a peccatis tuis in nomine patris, filii,
spiritus sancti. Amen."

The file of novices started toward the altar. The stained lights from the windows mingled with the candle glow and the eucharist in its golden halo seemed to the man very mystical and sweet. It was very calm. The subdeacon held the Book for him. He placed his right hand upon it.

"In the name of the Father and the Son and of the Holy Ghost—"

TARQUIN OF CHEAPSIDE

First published in
Nassau Literary Magazine, April, 1917

I

Running footsteps—light, soft-soled shoes made of curious leathery cloth brought from Ceylon setting the pace; thick flowing boots, two pairs, dark blue and gilt, reflecting the moonlight in blunt gleams and splotches, following a stone's throw behind.

Soft Shoes flashes through a patch of moonlight, then darts into a blind labyrinth of alleys and becomes only an intermittent scuffle ahead somewhere in the enfolding darkness. In go Flowing Boots, with short swords lurching and long plumes awry, finding a breath to curse God and the black lanes of London.

Soft Shoes leaps a shadowy gate and crackles through a hedgerow. Flowing Boots leap the gate and crackles through the hedgerow—and there, startlingly, is the watch ahead—two murderous pikemen of ferocious cast of mouth acquired in Holland and the Spanish marches.

But there is no cry for help. The pursued does not fall panting at the feet of the watch, clutching a purse; neither do the pursuers raise a hue and cry. Soft Shoes goes by in a rush of swift air. The watch curse and hesitate, glance after the fugitive, and then spread their pikes grimly across the road and wait for Flowing Boots. Darkness, like a great hand, cuts off the even flow the moon.

The hand moves off the moon whose pale caress finds again the eaves and lintels, and the watch, wounded and tumbled in the dust. Up the street one of Flowing Boots leaves a black trail of spots until he binds himself, clumsily as he runs, with fine lace caught from his throat.

It was no affair for the watch: Satan was at large tonight and Satan seemed to be he who appeared dimly in front, heel over gate, knee over fence. Moreover, the adversary was obviously travelling near home or at least in that section of London consecrated to his coarser whims, for the street narrowed like a road in a picture and the houses bent over further and further, cooping in natural ambushes suitable for murder and its histrionic sister, sudden death.

Down long and sinuous lanes twisted the hunted and the harriers, always in and out of the moon in a perpetual queen's move over a checker-board of glints and patches. Ahead, the quarry, minus his leather jerkin now and half blinded by drips of sweat, had taken to scanning his ground desperately on both sides. As a result he suddenly slowed short, and retracing his steps a bit scooted up an alley so dark that it seemed that here sun and moon had been in eclipse since the last glacier slipped roaring over the earth. Two hundred yards down he stopped and crammed himself into a niche in the wall where he huddled and panted silently, a grotesque god without bulk or outline in the gloom.

Flowing Boots, two pairs, drew near, came up, went by, halted twenty yards beyond him, and spoke in deep-lunged, scanty whispers:

"I was attune to that scuffle; it stopped."

"Within twenty paces."

"He's hid."

"Stay together now and we'll cut him up."

The voice faded into a low crunch of a boot, nor did Soft Shoes wait to hear more—he sprang in three leaps across the alley, where he bounded up, flapped for a moment on the top of the wall like a huge bird, and disappeared, gulped down by the hungry night at a mouthful.

II

"He read at wine, he read in bed,
He read aloud, had he the breath,
His every thought was with the dead,
And so he read himself to death."

Any visitor to the old James the First graveyard near Peat's Hill may spell out this bit of doggerel, undoubtedly one of the worst recorded of an Elizabethan, on the tomb of Wessel Caster.

This death of his, says the antiquary, occurred when he was thirty-seven, but as this story is concerned with the night of a certain chase through darkness, we find him still alive, still reading. His eyes were somewhat dim, his stomach somewhat obvious—he was a mis-built man and indolent—oh, Heavens! But an era is an era, and in the reign of Elizabeth, by the grace of Luther, Queen of England, no man could help but catch the spirit of enthusiasm. Every loft in Cheapside published its *Magnum Folium* (or magazine)—of its new blank verse; the Cheapside Players would produce anything on sight as long as it "got away from those reactionary miracle plays," and the English Bible had run through seven "very large" printings in as many months.

So Wessel Caxter (who in his youth had gone to sea) was now a reader of all on which he could lay his hands—he read manuscripts in holy friendship; he dined rotten poets; he loitered about the shops where the *Magna Folia* were printed, and he listened tolerantly while the young playwrights wrangled and bickered among them-selves, and behind each other's backs made bitter and malicious charges of plagiarism or anything else they could think of.

To-night he had a book, a piece of work which, though inordinately versed, contained, he thought, some rather excellent political satire. "The Faerie Queene" by Edmund Spenser lay before him under the tremulous candle-light. He had ploughed through a canto; he was beginning another:

THE LEGEND OF BRITOMARTIS OR OF CHASTITY

It falls me here to write of Chastity.
The fayrest vertue, far above the rest . . .

A sudden rush of feet on the stairs, a rusty swing-open of the thin door, and a man thrust himself into the room, a man without a jerkin, panting, sobbing, on the verge of collapse.

"Wessel," words choked him, "stick me away somewhere, love of Our Lady!"

Caxter rose, carefully closing his book, and bolted the door in some concern.

"I'm pursued," cried out Soft Shoes. "I vow there's two short-witted blades trying to make me into mincemeat and near succeeding. They saw me hop the back wall!"

"It would need," said Wessel, looking at him curiously, "several battalions armed with blunderbusses, and two or three Armadas, to keep you reasonably secure from the revenges of the world."

Soft Shoes smiled with satisfaction. His sobbing gasps were giving way to quick, precise breathing; his hunted air had faded to a faintly perturbed irony.

"I feel little surprise," continued Wessel.

"They were two such dreary apes."

"Making a total of three."

"Only two unless you stick me away. Man, man, come alive, they'll be on the stairs in a spark's age."

Wessel took a dismantled pike-staff from the corner, and raising it to the high ceiling, dislodged a rough trap-door opening into a garret above.

"There's no ladder."

He moved a bench under the trap, upon which Soft Shoes mounted, crouched, hesitated, crouched again, and then leaped amazingly upward. He caught at the edge of the aperture and swung back and forth, for a moment, shifting his hold; finally doubled up and disappeared into the darkness above. There was a scurry, a migration of rats, as the trap-door was replaced; . . . . silence.

Wessel returned to his reading-table, opened to the Legend of Britomartis or of Chastity—and waited. Almost a minute later there was a scramble on the stairs and an intolerable hammering at the door. Wessel sighed and, picking up his candle, rose.

"Who's there?"

"Open the door!"

"Who's there?"

An aching blow frightened the frail wood, splintered it around the edge. Wessel opened it a scarce three inches, and held the candle high. His was to play the timorous, the super-respectable citizen, disgracefully disturbed.

"One small hour of the night for rest. Is that too much to ask from every brawler and—"

"Quiet, gossip! Have you seen a perspiring fellow?"

The shadows of two gallants fell in immense wavering outlines over the narrow stairs; by the light Wessel scrutinized them closely. Gentlemen, they were, hastily but richly dressed—one of them wounded severely in the hand, both radiating a sort of furious horror. Waving aside Wessel's ready miscomprehension, they pushed by him into the room and with their swords went through the business of poking carefully into all suspected dark spots in the room, further extending their search to Wessel's bedchamber.

"Is he hid here?" demanded the wounded man fiercely.

"Is who here?"

"Any man but you."

"Only two others that I know of."

For a second Wessel feared that he had been too damned funny, for the gallants made as though to prick him through.

"I heard a man on the stairs," he said hastily, "full five minutes ago, it was. He most certainly failed to come up."

He went on to explain his absorption in "The Faerie Queene" but, for the moment at least, his visitors, like the great saints, were anaesthetic to culture.

"What's been done?" inquired Wessel.

"Violence!" said the man with the wounded hand. Wessel noticed that his eyes were quite wild. "My own sister. Oh, Christ in heaven, give us this man!"

Wessel winced.

"Who is the man?"

"God's word! We know not even that. What's that trap up there?" he added suddenly.

"It's nailed down. It's not been used for years." He thought of the pole in the corner and quailed in his belly, but the utter despair of the two men dulled their astuteness.

"It would take a ladder for any one not a tumbler," said the wounded man listlessly.

His companion broke into hysterical laughter.

"A tumbler. Oh, a tumbler. Oh—"

Wessel stared at them in wonder.

"That appeals to my most tragic humor," cried the man, "that no one—oh, no one—could get up there but a tumbler."

The gallant with the wounded hand snapped his good fingers impatiently.

"We must go next door—and then on—"

Helplessly they went as two walking under a dark and storm-swept sky.

Wessel closed and bolted the door and stood a moment by it, frowning in pity.

A low-breathed "Ha!" made him look up. Soft Shoes had already raised the trap and was looking down into the room, his rather elfish face squeezed into a grimace, half of distaste, half of sardonic amusement.

"They take off their heads with their helmets," he remarked in a whisper, "but as for you and me, Wessel, we are two cunning men."

"Now you be cursed," cried Wessel vehemently. "I knew you for a dog, but when I hear even the half of a tale like this, I know you for such a dirty cur that I am minded to club your skull."

Soft Shoes stared at him, blinking.

"At all events," he replied finally, "I find dignity impossible in this position."

With this he let his body through the trap, hung for an instant, and dropped the seven feet to the floor.

"There was a rat considered my ear with the air of a gourmet," he continued, dusting his hands on his breeches. "I told him in the rat's peculiar idiom that I was deadly poison, so he took himself off."

"Let's hear of this night's lechery!" insisted Wessel angrily.

Soft Shoes touched his thumb to his nose and wiggled the fingers derisively at Wessel.

"Street gamin!" muttered Wessel.

"Have you any paper?" demanded Soft Shoes irrelevantly, and then rudely added, "or can you write?"

"Why should I give you paper?"

"You wanted to hear of the night's entertainment. So you shall, an you give me pen, ink, a sheaf of paper, and a room to myself."

Wessel hesitated.

"Get out!" he said finally.

"As you will. Yet you have missed a most intriguing story."

Wessel wavered—he was soft as taffy, that man—gave in. Soft Shoes went into the adjoining room with the begrudged writing materials and precisely closed the door. Wessel grunted and returned to "The Faerie Queene"; so silence came once more upon the house.

III

Three o'clock went into four. The room paled, the dark outside was shot through with damp and chill, and Wessel, cupping his brain in his hands, bent low over his table, tracing through the pattern of knights and fairies and the harrowing distresses of many girls. There were dragons chortling along the narrow street outside; when the sleepy armorer's boy began his work at half-past five the heavy clink and clank of plate and linked mail swelled to the echo of a marching cavalcade.

A fog shut down at the first flare of dawn, and the room was grayish yellow at six when Wessel tiptoed to his cupboard bedchamber and pulled open the door. His guest turned on him a face pale as parchment in which two distraught eyes burned like great red letters. He had drawn a chair close to Wessel's *prie-dieu* which he was using as a desk; and on it was an amazing stack of closely written pages. With a long sigh Wessel withdrew and returned to his siren, calling himself fool for not claiming his bed here at dawn.

The clump of boots outside, the croaking of old beldames from attic to attic, the dull murmur of morning, unnerved him, and, dozing, he slumped in his chair, his brain, overladen with sound and color, working intolerably over the imagery that stacked it. In this restless dream of his he was one of a thousand groaning bodies crushed near the sun, a helpless bridge for the strong-eyed Apollo. The dream tore at him, scraped along his mind like a ragged knife. When a hot hand touched his shoulder, he awoke with what was nearly a scream to find the fog thick in the room and his guest, a gray ghost of misty stuff, beside him with a pile of paper in his hand.

"It should be a most intriguing tale, I believe, though it requires some going over. May I ask you to lock it away, and in God's name let me sleep?"

He waited for no answer, but thrust the pile at Wessel, and literally poured himself like stuff from a suddenly inverted bottle upon a couch in the corner; slept, with his breathing regular, but his brow wrinkled in a curious and somewhat uncanny manner.

Wessel yawned sleepily and, glancing at the scrawled, uncertain first page, he began reading aloud very softly:

THE RAPE OF LUCRECE

"From the besieged Ardea all in post,
Borne by the trustless wings of false desire,
Lust-breathing Tarquin leaves the Roman host—"

THE OFFSHORE PIRATE

First published in
The Saturday Evening Post, May, 1920

I

This unlikely story begins on a sea that was a blue dream, as colorful as blue-silk stockings, and beneath a sky as blue as the irises of children's eyes. From the western half of the sky the sun was shying little golden disks at the sea—if you gazed intently enough you could see them skip from wave tip to wave tip until they joined a broad collar of golden coin that was collecting half a mile out and would eventually be a dazzling sunset. About half-way between the Florida shore and the golden collar a white steam-yacht, very young and graceful, was riding at anchor and under a blue-and-white awning aft a yellow-haired girl reclined in a wicker settee reading The Revolt of the Angels, by Anatole France.

She was about nineteen, slender and supple, with a spoiled alluring mouth and quick gray eyes full of a radiant curiosity. Her feet, stockingless, and adorned rather than clad in blue-satin slippers which swung nonchalantly from her toes, were perched on the arm of a settee adjoining the one she occupied. And as she read she intermittently regaled herself by a faint application to her tongue of a half-lemon that she held in her hand. The other half, sucked dry, lay on the deck at her feet and rocked very gently to and fro at the almost imperceptible motion of the tide.

The second half-lemon was well-nigh pulpless and the golden collar had grown astonishing in width, when suddenly the drowsy silence which enveloped the yacht was broken by the sound of heavy footsteps and an elderly man topped with orderly gray hair and clad in a white-flannel suit appeared at the head of the companionway. There he paused for a moment until his eyes became accustomed to the sun, and then seeing the girl under the awning he uttered a long even grunt of disapproval.

If he had intended thereby to obtain a rise of any sort he was doomed to disappointment. The girl calmly turned over two pages, turned back one, raised the lemon mechanically to tasting distance, and then very faintly but quite unmistakably yawned.

"Ardita!" said the gray-haired man sternly.

Ardita uttered a small sound indicating nothing.

"Ardita!" he repeated. "Ardita!"

Ardita raised the lemon languidly, allowing three words to slip out before it reached her tongue.

"Oh, shut up."

"Ardita!"

"What?"

"Will you listen to me—or will I have to get a servant to hold you while I talk to you?"

The lemon descended very slowly and scornfully.

"Put it in writing."

"Will you have the decency to close that abominable book and discard that damn lemon for two minutes?"

"Oh, can't you lemme alone for a second?"

"Ardita, I have just received a telephone message from the shore——"

"Telephone?" She showed for the first time a faint interest.

"Yes, it was——"

"Do you mean to say," she interrupted wonderingly, "'at they let you run a wire out here?"

"Yes, and just now——"

"Won't other boats bump into it?"

"No. It's run along the bottom. Five min——"

"Well, I'll be darned! Gosh! Science is golden or something—isn't it?"

"Will you let me say what I started to?"

"Shoot!"

"Well it seems—well, I am up here—" He paused and swallowed several times distractedly. "Oh, yes. Young woman, Colonel Moreland has called up again to ask me to be sure to bring you in to dinner. His son Toby has come all the way from New York to meet you and he's invited several other young people. For the last time, will you——"

"No," said Ardita shortly, "I won't. I came along on this darn cruise with the one idea of going to Palm Beach, and you knew it, and I absolutely refuse to meet any darn old colonel or any darn young Toby or any darn old young people or to set foot in any other darn old town in this crazy state. So you either take me to Palm Beach or else shut up and go away."

"Very well. This is the last straw. In your infatuation for this man.—a man who is notorious for his excesses—a man your father would not have allowed to so much as mention your name—you have rejected the demi-monde rather than the circles in which you have presumably grown up. From now on——"

"I know," interrupted Ardita ironically, "from now on you go your way and I go mine. I've heard that story before. You know I'd like nothing better."

"From now on," he announced grandiloquently, "you are no niece of mine. I——"

"O-o-o-oh!" The cry was wrung from Ardita with the agony of a lost soul. "Will you stop boring me! Will you go 'way! Will you jump overboard and drown! Do you want me to throw this book at you!"

"If you dare do any——"

Smack! The Revolt of the Angels sailed through the air, missed its target by the length of a short nose, and bumped cheerfully down the companionway.

The gray-haired man made an instinctive step backward and then two cautious steps forward. Ardita jumped to her five feet four and stared at him defiantly, her gray eyes blazing.

"Keep off!"

"How dare you!" he cried.

"Because I darn please!"

"You've grown unbearable! Your disposition——"

"You've made me that way! No child ever has a bad disposition unless it's her fancy's fault! Whatever I am, you did it."

Muttering something under his breath her uncle turned and, walking forward called in a loud voice for the launch. Then he returned to the awning, where Ardita had again seated herself and resumed her attention to the lemon.

"I am going ashore," he said slowly. "I will be out again at nine o'clock to-night. When I return we start back to New York, wither I shall turn you over to your aunt for the rest of your natural, or rather unnatural, life." He paused and looked at her, and then all at once something in the utter childness of her beauty seemed to puncture his anger like an inflated tire, and render him helpless, uncertain, utterly fatuous.

"Ardita," he said not unkindly, "I'm no fool. I've been round. I know men. And, child, confirmed libertines don't reform until they're tired—and then they're not themselves—they're husks of themselves." He looked at her as if expecting agreement, but receiving no sight or sound of it he continued. "Perhaps the man loves you—that's possible. He's loved many women and he'll love many more. Less than a month ago, one month, Ardita, he was involved in a notorious affair with that red-haired woman, Mimi Merril; promised to give her the diamond bracelet that the Czar of Russia gave his mother. You know—you read the papers."

"Thrilling scandals by an anxious uncle," yawned Ardita. "Have it filmed. Wicked clubman making eyes at virtuous flapper. Virtuous flapper conclusively vamped by his lurid past. Plans to meet him at Palm Beach. Foiled by anxious uncle."

"Will you tell me why the devil you want to marry him?"

"I'm sure I couldn't say," said Audits shortly. "Maybe because he's the only man I know, good or bad, who has an imagination and the courage of his convictions. Maybe it's to get away from the young fools that spend their vacuous hours pursuing me around the country. But as for the famous Russian bracelet, you can set your mind at rest on that score. He's going to give it to me at Palm Beach—if you'll show a little intelligence."

"How about the—red-haired woman?"

"He hasn't seen her for six months," she said angrily. "Don't you suppose I have enough pride to see to that? Don't you know by this time that I can do any darn thing with any darn man I want to?"

She put her chin in the air like the statue of France Aroused, and then spoiled the pose somewhat by raising the lemon for action.

"Is it the Russian bracelet that fascinates you?"

"No, I'm merely trying to give you the sort of argument that would appeal to your intelligence. And I wish you'd go 'way," she said, her temper rising again. "You know I never change my mind. You've been boring me for three days until I'm about to go crazy. I won't go ashore! Won't! Do you hear? Won't!"

"Very well," he said, "and you won't go to Palm Beach either. Of all the selfish, spoiled, uncontrolled disagreeable, impossible girl I have——"

Splush! The half-lemon caught him in the neck. Simultaneously came a hail from over the side.

"The launch is ready, Mr. Farnam."

Too full of words and rage to speak, Mr. Farnam cast one utterly condemning glance at his niece and, turning, ran swiftly down the ladder.

II

Five o'clock robed down from the sun and plumped soundlessly into the sea. The golden collar widened into a glittering island; and a faint breeze that had been playing with the edges of the awning and swaying one of the dangling blue slippers became suddenly freighted with song. It was a chorus of men in close harmony and in perfect rhythm to an accompanying sound of oars dealing the blue writers. Ardita lifted her head and listened.

> "Carrots and Peas,
> Beans on their knees,
> Pigs in the seas,
>   Lucky fellows!
> Blow us a breeze,
> Blow us a breeze,
> Blow us a breeze,
>   With your bellows."

Ardita's brow wrinkled in astonishment. Sitting very still she listened eagerly as the chorus took up a second verse.

> "Onions and beans,
> Marshalls and Deans,
> Goldbergs and Greens
>   And Costellos.
> Blow us a breeze,
> Blow us a breeze,
> Blow us a breeze,
>   With your bellows."

With an exclamation she tossed her book to the desk, where it sprawled at a straddle, and hurried to the rail. Fifty feet away a large rowboat was approaching containing seven men, six of

them rowing and one standing up in the stern keeping time to
their song with an orchestra leader's baton.

>"Oysters and Rocks,
>Sawdust and socks,
>Who could make clocks
>   Out of cellos?——"

The leader's eyes suddenly rested on Ardita, who was leaning
over the rail spellbound with curiosity. He made a quick
movement with his baton and the singing instantly ceased. She
saw that he was the only white man in the boat—the six rowers
were negroes.

"Narcissus ahoy!" he called politely.

"What's the idea of all the discord?" demanded Ardita
cheerfully. "Is this the varsity crew from the county nut farm?"

By this time the boat was scraping the side of the yacht and
a great bulking negro in the bow turned round and grasped the
ladder. Thereupon the leader left his position in the stern and
before Ardita had realized his intention he ran up the ladder and
stood breathless before her on the deck.

"The women and children will be spared!" he said briskly.
"All crying babies will be immediately drowned and all males
put in double irons!" Digging her hands excitedly down into
the pockets of her dress Ardita stared at him, speechless with
astonishment. He was a young man with a scornful mouth and
the bright blue eyes of a healthy baby set in a dark sensitive face.
His hair was pitch black, damp and curly—the hair of a Grecian
statue gone brunette. He was trimly built, trimly dressed, and
graceful as an agile quarter-back.

"Well, I'll be a son of a gun!" she said dazedly.

They eyed each other coolly.

"Do you surrender the ship?"

"Is this an outburst of wit?" demanded Ardita. "Are you an
idiot—or just being initiated to some fraternity?"

"I asked you if you surrendered the ship."

"I thought the country was dry," said Ardita disdainfully. "Have you been drinking finger-nail enamel? You better get off this yacht!"

"What?" the young man's voice expressed incredulity.

"Get off the yacht! You heard me!"

He looked at her for a moment as if considering what she had said.

"No," said his scornful mouth slowly; "No, I won't get off the yacht. You can get off if you wish."

Going to the rail be gave a curt command and immediately the crew of the rowboat scrambled up the ladder and ranged themselves in line before him, a coal-black and burly darky at one end and a miniature mulatto of four feet nine at to other. They seemed to be uniformly dressed in some sort of blue costume ornamented with dust, mud, and tatters; over the shoulder of each was slung a small, heavy-looking white sack, and under their arms they carried large black cases apparently containing musical instruments.

"'Ten-*shun*!" commanded the young man, snapping his own heels together crisply. "Right *driss*! Front! Step out here, Babe!"

The smallest Negro took a quick step forward and saluted.

"Take command, go down below, catch the crew and tie 'em up—all except the engineer. Bring him up to me. Oh, and pile those bags by the rail there."

"Yas-suh!"

Babe saluted again and wheeling about motioned for the five others to gather about him. Then after a short whispered consultation they all filed noiselessly down the companionway.

"Now," said the young man cheerfully to Ardita, who had witnessed this last scene in withering silence, "if you will swear on your honor as a flapper—which probably isn't worth much—that you'll keep that spoiled little mouth of yours tight shut for forty-eight hours, you can row yourself ashore in our rowboat."

"Otherwise what?"

"Otherwise you're going to sea in a ship."

With a little sigh as for a crisis well passed, the young man sank into the settee Ardita had lately vacated and stretched his arms lazily. The corners of his mouth relaxed appreciatively as he looked round at the rich striped awning, the polished brass, and the luxurious fittings of the deck. His eye felt on the book, and then on the exhausted lemon.

"Hm," he said, "Stonewall Jackson claimed that lemon-juice cleared his head. Your head feel pretty clear?"

Ardita disdained to answer.

"Because inside of five minutes you'll have to make a clear decision whether it's go or stay."

He picked up the book and opened it curiously.

"The Revolt of the Angels. Sounds pretty good. French, eh?" He stared at her with new interest "You French?"

"No."

"What's your name?"

"Farnam."

"Farnam what?"

"Ardita Farnam."

"Well Ardita, no use standing up there and chewing out the insides of your mouth. You ought to break those nervous habits while you're young. Come over here and sit down."

Ardita took a carved jade case from her pocket, extracted a cigarette and lit it with a conscious coolness, though she knew her hand was trembling a little; then she crossed over with her supple, swinging walk, and sitting down in the other settee blew a mouthful of smoke at the awning.

"You can't get me off this yacht," she raid steadily; "and you haven't got very much sense if you think you'll get far with it. My uncle'll have wirelesses zigzagging all over this ocean by half past six."

"Hm."

She looked quickly at his face, caught anxiety stamped there plainly in the faintest depression of the mouth's corners.

"It's all the same to me," she said, shrugging her shoulders. "'Tisn't my yacht. I don't mind going for a coupla hours' cruise. I'll even lend you that book so you'll have something to read on the revenue boat that takes you up to Sing-Sing."

He laughed scornfully.

"If that's advice you needn't bother. This is part of a plan arranged before I ever knew this yacht existed. If it hadn't been this one it'd have been the next one we passed anchored along the coast."

"Who are you?" demanded Ardita suddenly. "And what are you?"

"You've decided not to go ashore?"

"I never even faintly considered it."

"We're generally known," he said "all seven of us, as Curtis Carlyle and his Six Black Buddies late of the Winter Garden and the Midnight Frolic."

"You're singers?"

"We were until to-day. At present, due to those white bags you see there we're fugitives from justice and if the reward offered for our capture hasn't by this time reached twenty thousand dollars I miss my guess."

"What's in the bags?" asked Ardita curiously.

"Well," he said "for the present we'll call it—mud—Florida mud."

III

Within ten minutes after Curtis Carlyle's interview with a very frightened engineer the yacht Narcissus was under way, steaming south through a balmy tropical twilight. The little mulatto, Babe, who seems to have Carlyle's implicit confidence, took full command of the situation. Mr. Farnam's valet and the chef, the only members of the crew on board except the engineer, having shown fight, were now reconsidering, strapped securely to their bunks below. Trombone Mose, the biggest negro, was set busy with a can of paint obliterating the name Narcissus from the bow, and substituting the name Hula Hula, and the others congregated aft and became intently involved in a game of craps.

Having given order for a meal to be prepared and served on deck at seven-thirty, Carlyle rejoined Ardita, and, sinking back into his settee, half closed his eyes and fell into a state of profound abstraction.

Ardita scrutinized him carefully—and classed him immediately as a romantic figure. He gave the effect of towering self-confidence erected on a slight foundation—just under the surface of each of his decisions she discerned a hesitancy that was in decided contrast to the arrogant curl of his lips.

"He's not like me," she thought "There's a difference somewhere." Being a supreme egotist Ardita frequently thought about herself; never having had her egotism disputed she did it entirely naturally and with no detraction from her unquestioned charm. Though she was nineteen she gave the effect of a high-spirited precocious child, and in the present glow of her youth and beauty all the men and women she had known were but driftwood on the ripples of her temperament. She had met other egotists—in fact she found that selfish people bored her rather less than unselfish people—but as yet there had not been one she had not eventually defeated and brought to her feet.

But though she recognized an egotist in the settee, she felt none of that usual shutting of doors in her mind which meant clearing ship for action; on the contrary her instinct told her that this man was somehow completely pregnable and quite defenseless. When Ardita defied convention—and of late it had been her chief amusement—it was from an intense desire to be herself, and she felt that this man, on the contrary, was preoccupied with his own defiance.

She was much more interested in him than she was in her own situation, which affected her as the prospect of a matineé might affect a ten-year-old child. She had implicit confidence in her ability to take care of herself under any and all circumstances.

The night deepened. A pale new moon smiled misty-eyed upon the sea, and as the shore faded dimly out and dark clouds were blown like leaves along the far horizon a great haze of moonshine suddenly bathed the yacht and spread an avenue of glittering mail in her swift path. From time to time there was the bright flare of a match as one of them lighted a cigarette, but except for the low under-tone of the throbbing engines and the even wash of the waves about the stern the yacht was quiet as a dream boat star-bound through the heavens. Round them bowed the smell of the night sea, bringing with it an infinite languor.

Carlyle broke the silence at last.

"Lucky girl," he sighed "I've always wanted to be rich—and buy all this beauty."

Ardita yawned.

"I'd rather be you," she said frankly.

"You would—for about a day. But you do seem to possess a lot of nerve for a flapper."

"I wish you wouldn't call me that."

"Beg your pardon."

"As to nerve," she continued slowly, "it's my one redeemiug feature. I'm not afraid of anything in heaven or earth."

"Hm, I am."

"To be afraid," said Ardita, "a person has either to be very great and strong—or else a coward. I'm neither." She paused for a moment, and eagerness crept into her tone. "But I want to talk about you. What on earth have you done—and how did you do it?"

"Why?" he demanded cynically. "Going to write a movie, about me?"

"Go on," she urged. "Lie to me by the moonlight. Do a fabulous story."

A negro appeared, switched on a string of small lights under the awning, and began setting the wicker table for supper. And while they ate cold sliced chicken, salad, artichokes and strawberry jam from the plentiful larder below, Carlyle began to talk, hesitatingly at first, but eagerly as he saw she was interested. Ardita scarcely touched her food as she watched his dark young face—handsome, ironic faintly ineffectual.

He began life as a poor kid in a Tennessee town, he said, so poor that his people were the only white family in their street. He never remembered any white children—but there were inevitably a dozen pickaninnies streaming in his trail, passionate admirers whom he kept in tow by the vividness of his imagination and the amount of trouble he was always getting them in and out of. And it seemed that this association diverted a rather unusual musical gift into a strange channel.

There had been a colored woman named Belle Pope Calhoun who played the piano at parties given for white children—nice white children that would have passed Curtis Carlyle with a sniff. But the ragged little "poh white" used to sit beside her piano by the hour and try to get in an alto with one of those kazoos that boys hum through. Before he was thirteen he was picking up a living teasing ragtime out of a battered violin in little cafés round Nashville. Eight years later the ragtime craze hit the country, and he took six darkies on the Orpheum circuit. Five of them were boys he had grown up with; the other was the little mulatto, Babe Divine, who was a wharf nigger round New York, and long before that a plantation hand in Bermuda, until he stuck an eight-inch stiletto in his master's back. Almost before Carlyle realized his good fortune he was on Broadway, with offers of engagements on all sides, and more money than he had ever dreamed of.

It was about then that a change began in his whole attitude, a rather curious, embittering change. It was when he realized that he was spending the golden years of his life gibbering round a stage with a lot of black men. His act was good of its kind—three trombones, three saxophones, and Carlyle's flute—and it was his own peculiar sense of rhythm that made all the difference; but he began to grow strangely sensitive about it, began to hate the thought of appearing, dreaded it from day to day.

They were making money—each contract he signed called for more—but when he went to managers and told them that he wanted to separate from his sextet and go on as a regular pianist, they laughed at him and told him he was crazy—it would be an artistic suicide. He used to laugh afterward at the phrase "artistic suicide." They all used it.

Half a dozen times they played at private dances at three thousand dollars a night, and it seemed as if these crystallized all his distaste for his mode of livlihood. They took place in clubs and houses that he couldn't have gone into in the daytime. After all, he was merely playing to rôle of the eternal monkey, a sort of sublimated chorus man. He was sick of the very smell of the theatre, of powder and rouge and the chatter of the greenroom, and the patronizing approval of the boxes. He couldn't put his heart into it any more. The idea of a slow approach to the luxury of leisure drove him wild. He was, of course, progressing toward it, but, like a child, eating his ice-cream so slowly that he couldn't taste it at all.

He wanted to have a lot of money and time and opportunity to read and play, and the sort of men and women round him that he could never have—the kind who, if they thought of him at all, would have considered him rather contemptible; in short he wanted all those things which he was beginning to lump under the general head of aristocracy, an aristocracy which it seemed almost any money could buy except money made as he was making it. He was twenty-five then, without family or education or any promise that he would succeed in a business career. He began speculating wildly, and within three weeks he had lost every cent he had saved.

Then the war came. He went to Plattsburg, and even there his profession followed him. A brigadier-general called him up to headquarters and told him he could serve his country better as a band leader—so he spent the war entertaining celebrities behind the line with a headquarters band. It was not so bad—except that when the infantry came limping back from the trenches he wanted to be one of them. The sweat and mud they wore seemed only one of those ineffable symbols of aristocracy that were forever eluding him.

"It was the private dances that did it. After I came back from the war the old routine started. We had an offer from a syndicate of Florida hotels. It was only a question of time then."

He broke off and Ardita looked at him expectantly, but he shook his head.

"No," he said, "I'm going to tell you about it. I'm enjoying it too much, and I'm afraid I'd lose a little of that enjoyment if I shared it with anyone else. I want to hang on to those few breathless, heroic moments when I stood out before them all and let them know I was more than a damn bobbing, squawking clown."

From up forward came suddenly the low sound of singing. The negroes had gathered together on the deck and their voices rose together in a haunting melody that soared in poignant harmonics toward the moon. And Ardita listens in enchantment.

"Oh down——
　　oh down,
Mammy wanna take me down milky way,
Oh down,
　　oh down,
Pappy say to-morra-a-a-ah
But mammy say to-day,
Yes—mammy say to-day!"

Carlyle sighed and was silent for a moment looking up at the gathered host of stars blinking like arc-lights in the warm sky. The negroes' song had died away to a plaintive humming and it seemed as if minute by minute the brightness and the great silence were increasing until he could almost hear the midnight toilet of the mermaids as they combed their silver dripping curls under the moon and gossiped to each other of the fine wrecks they lived on the green opalescent avenues below.

"You see," said Carlyle softly, "this is the beauty I want. Beauty has got to be astonishing, astounding—it's got to burst in on you like a dream, like the exquisite eyes of a girl."

He turned to her, but she was silent.

"You see, don't you, Anita—I mean, Ardita?"

Again she made no answer. She had been sound asleep for some time.

IV

In the dense sun-flooded noon of next day a spot in the sea before them resolved casually into a green-and-gray islet, apparently composed of a great granite cliff at its northern end which slanted south through a mile of vivid coppice and grass to a sandy beach melting lazily into the surf. When Ardita, reading in her favorite seat, came to the last page of The Revolt of the Angels, and slamming the book shut looked up and saw it, she gave a little cry of delight, and called to Carlyle, who was standing moodily by the rail.

"Is this it? Is this where you're going?"

Carlyle shrugged his shoulders carelessly.

"You've got me." He raised his voice and called up to the acting skipper: "Oh, Babe, is this your island?"

The mulatto's miniature head appeared from round the corner of the deck-house.

"Yas-suh! This yeah's it."

Carlyle joined Ardita.

"Looks sort of sporting, doesn't it?"

"Yes," she agreed; "but it doesn't look big enough to be much of a hiding-place."

"You still putting your faith in those wirelesses your uncle was going to have zigzagging round?"

"No," said Ardita frankly. "I'm all for you. I'd really like to see you make a get-away."

He laughed.

"You're our Lady Luck. Guess we'll have to keep you with us as a mascot—for the present anyway."

"You couldn't very well ask me to swim back," she said coolly. "If you do I'm going to start writing dime novels founded on that interminable history of your life you gave me last night."

He flushed and stiffened slightly.

"I'm very sorry I bored you."

"Oh, you didn't—until just at the end with some story about how furious you were because you couldn't dance with the ladies you played music for."

He rose angrily.

"You have got a darn mean little tongue."

"Excuse me," she said melting into laughter, "but I'm not used to having men regale me with the story of their life ambitions— especially if they've lived such deathly platonic lives."

"Why? What do men usually regale you with?"

"Oh, they talk about me," she yawned. "They tell me I'm the spirit of youth and beauty."

"What do you tell them?"

"Oh, I agree quietly."

"Does every man you meet tell you he loves you?"

Ardita nodded.

"Why shouldn't he? All life is just a progression toward, and then a recession from, one phrase—'I love you.'"

Carlyle laughed and sat down.

"That's very true. That's—that's not bad. Did you make that up?"

"Yes—or rather I found it out. It doesn't mean anything especially. It's just clever."

"It's the sort of remark," he said gravely, "that's typical of your class."

"Oh," she interrupted impatiently, "don't start that lecture on aristocracy again! I distrust people who can be intense at this hour in the morning. It's a mild form of insanity—a sort of breakfast-food jag. Morning's the time to sleep, swim, and be careless."

Ten minutes later they had swung round in a wide circle as if to approach the island from the north.

"There's a trick somewhere," commented Ardita thoughtfully. "He can't mean just to anchor up against this cliff."

They were heading straight in now toward the solid rock, which must have been well over a hundred feet tall, and not until they were within fifty yards of it did Ardita see their objective. Then she clapped her hands in delight. There was a break in the cliff entirely hidden by a curious overlapping of rock, and through this break the yacht entered and very slowly traversed a narrow channel of crystal-clear water between high gray walls. Then they were riding at anchor in a miniature world of green and gold, a gilded bay smooth as glass and set round with tiny palms, the whole resembling the mirror lakes and twig trees that children set up in sand piles.

"Not so darned bad!" cried Carlyle excitedly.

"I guess that little coon knows his way round this corner of the Atlantic."

His exuberance was contagious, and Ardita became quite jubilant.

"It's an absolutely sure-fire hiding-place!"

"Lordy, yes! It's the sort of island you read about."

The rowboat was lowered into the golden lake and they pulled to shore.

"Come on," said Carlyle as they landed in the slushy sand, "we'll go exploring."

The fringe of palms was in turn ringed in by a round mile of flat, sandy country. They followed it south and brushing through a farther rim of tropical vegetation came out on a pearl-gray virgin beach where Ardita kicked of her brown golf shoes—she seemed to have permanently abandoned stockings—and went wading. Then they sauntered back to the yacht, where the indefatigable Babe had luncheon ready for them. He had posted a lookout on the high cliff to the north to watch the sea on both sides, though he doubted if the entrance to the cliff was generally known—he had never even seen a map on which the island was marked.

"What's its name," asked Ardita—"the island, I mean?"

"No name 'tall," chuckled Babe. "Reckin she jus' island, 'at's all."

In the late afternoon they sat with their backs against great boulders on the highest part of the cliff and Carlyle sketched for her his vague plans. He was sure they were hot after him by this time. The total proceeds of the coup he had pulled off and concerning which he still refused to enlighten her, he estimated as just under a million dollars. He counted on lying up here several weeks and then setting off southward, keeping well outside the usual channels of travel rounding the Horn and heading for Callao, in Peru. The details of coaling and provisioning he was leaving entirely to Babe who, it seemed, had sailed these seas in every capacity from cabin-boy aboard a coffee trader to virtual first mate on a Brazillian pirate craft, whose skipper had long since been hung.

"If he'd been white he'd have been king of South America long ago," said Carlyle emphatically. "When it comes to intelligence he makes Booker T. Washington look like a moron. He's got the guile of every race and nationality whose blood is in his veins, and that's half a dozen or I'm a liar. He worships me because I'm the only man in the world who can play better ragtime than he can. We used to sit together on the wharfs down on the New York water-front, he with a bassoon and me with an oboe, and we'd blend minor keys in African harmonics a thousand years old until the rats would crawl up the posts and sit round groaning and squeaking like dogs will in front of a phonograph."

Ardita roared.

"How you can tell 'em!"

Carlyle grinned.

"I swear that's the gos——"

"What you going to do when you get to Callao?" she interrupted.

"Take ship for India. I want to be a rajah. I mean it. My idea is to go up into Afghanistan somewhere, buy up a palace and a reputation, and then after about five years appear in England with a foreign accent and a mysterious past. But India first. Do you know, they say that all the gold in the world drifts very gradually back to India. Something fascinating about that to me. And I want leisure to read—an immense amount."

"How about after that?"

"Then," he answered defiantly, "comes aristocracy. Laugh if you want to—but at least you'll have to admit that I know what I want—which I imagine is more than you do."

"On the contrary," contradicted Ardita, reaching in her pocket for her cigarette case, "when I met you I was in the midst of a great uproar of all my friends and relatives because I did know what I wanted."

"What was it?"

"A man."

He started.

"You mean you were engaged?"

"After a fashion. If you hadn't come aboard I had every intention of slipping ashore yesterday evening—how long ago it seems—and meeting him in Palm Beach. He's waiting there for me with a bracelet that once belonged to Catherine of Russia. Now don't mutter anything about aristocracy," she put in quickly. "I liked him simply because he had had an imagination and the utter courage of his convictions."

"But your family disapproved, eh?"

"What there is of it—only a silly uncle and a sillier aunt. It seems he got into some scandal with a red-haired woman name Mimi something—it was frightfully exaggerated, he said, and men don't lie to me—and anyway I didn't care what he'd done; it was the future that counted. And I'd see to that. When a man's in love with me he doesn't care for other amusements. I told him to drop her like a hot cake, and he did."

"I feel rather jealous," said Carlyle, frowning—and then he laughed. "I guess I'll just keep you along with us until we get to Callao. Then I'll lend you enough money to get back to the States. By that time you'll have had a chance to think that gentleman over a little more."

"Don't talk to me like that!" fired up Ardita. "I won't tolerate the parental attitude from anybody! Do you understand me?" He chuckled and then stopped, rather abashed, as her cold anger seemed to fold him about and chill him.

"I'm sorry," he offered uncertainly.

"Oh, don't apologize! I can't stand men who say 'I'm sorry' in that manly, reserved tone. Just shut up!"

A pause ensued, a pause which Carlyle found rather awkward, but which Ardita seemed not to notice at all as she sat contentedly enjoying her cigarette and gazing out at the shining sea. After a minute she crawled out on the rock and lay with her face over the edge looking down. Carlyle, watching her, reflected how it seemed impossible for her to assume an ungraceful attitude.

"Oh, look," she cried. "There's a lot of sort of ledges down there. Wide ones of all different heights."

"We'll go swimming to-night!" she said excitedly. "By moonlight."

"Wouldn't you rather go in at the beach on the other end?"

"Not a chance. I like to dive. You can use my uncle's bathing suit, only it'll fit you like a gunny sack, because he's a very flabby man. I've got a one-piece that's shocked the natives all along the Atlantic coast from Biddeford Pool to St. Augustine."

"I suppose you're a shark."

"Yes, I'm pretty good. And I look cute too. A sculptor up at Rye last summer told me my calves are worth five hundred dollars."

There didn't seem to be any answer to this, so Carlyle was silent, permitting himself only a discreet interior smile.

V

When the night crept down in shadowy blue and silver they threaded the shimmering channel in the rowboat and, tying it to a jutting rock, began climbing the cliff together. The first shelf was ten feet up, wide, and furnishing a natural diving platform. There they sat down in the bright moonlight and watched the faint incessant surge of the waters almost stilled now as the tide set seaward.

"Are you happy?" he asked suddenly.

She nodded.

"Always happy near the sea. You know," she went on, "I've been thinking all day that you and I are somewhat alike. We're both rebels—only for different reasons. Two years ago, when I was just eighteen and you were——"

"Twenty-five."

"——well, we were both conventional successes. I was an utterly devastating débutante and you were a prosperous musician just commissioned in the army——"

"Gentleman by act of Congress," he put in ironically.

"Well, at any rate, we both fitted. If our corners were not rubbed off they were at least pulled in. But deep in us both was something that made us require more for happiness. I didn't know what I wanted. I went from man to man, restless, impatient, month by month getting less acquiescent and more dissatisfied. I used to sit sometimes chewing at the insides of my mouth and thinking I was going crazy—I had a frightful sense of transiency. I wanted things now—now—now! Here I was— beautiful—I am, aren't I?"

"Yes," agreed Carlyle tentatively.

Ardita rose suddenly.

"Wait a second. I want to try this delightful-looking sea."

She walked to the end of the ledge and shot out over the sea, doubling up in mid-air and then straightening out and entering to water straight as a blade in a perfect jack-knife dive.

In a minute her voice floated up to him.

"You see, I used to read all day and most of the night. I began to resent society——"

"Come on up here," he interrupted. "What on earth are you doing?"

"Just floating round on my back. I'll be up in a minute. Let me tell you. The only thing I enjoyed was shocking people; wearing something quite impossible and quite charming to a fancy-dress party, going round with the fastest men in New York, and getting into some of the most hellish scrapes imaginable."

The sounds of splashing mingled with her words, and then he heard her hurried breathing as she began climbing up side to the ledge.

"Go on in!" she called

Obediently he rose and dived. When he emerged, dripping, and made the climb he found that she was no longer on the ledge, but after a second frightened he heard her light laughter from another shelf ten feet up. There he joined her and they both sat quietly for a moment, their arms clasped round their knees, panting a little from the climb.

"The family were wild," she said suddenly. "They tried to marry me off. And then when I'd begun to feel that after all life was scarcely worth living I found something"—her eyes went skyward exultantly——"I found something!"

Carlyle waited and her words came with a rush.

"Courage—just that; courage as a rule of life, and something to cling to always. I began to build up this enormous faith in myself. I began to see that in all my idols in the past some manifestation of courage had unconsciously been the thing that attracted me. I began separating courage from the other things of life. All sorts of courage—the beaten, bloody prize-fighter coming up for more—I used to make men take me to prize-fights; the déclassé woman sailing through a nest of cats and looking at them as if they were mud under her feet; the liking what you like always; the utter disregard for other people's opinions—just to live as I liked always and to die in my own way— Did you bring up the cigarettes?"

He handed one over and held a match for her gently.

"Still," Ardita continued, "the men kept gathering—old men and young men, my mental and physical inferiors, most of them, but all intensely desiring to have me—to own this rather magnificent proud tradition I'd built up round me. Do you see?"

"Sort of. You never were beaten and you never apologized."

"Never!"

She sprang to the edge, poised for a moment like a crucified figure against the sky; then describing a dark parabola plunked without a slash between two silver ripples twenty feet below.

Her voice floated up to him again.

"And courage to me meant ploughing through that dull gray mist that comes down on life—not only overriding people and circumstances but overriding the bleakness of living. A sort of insistence on the value of life and the worth of transient things."

She was climbing up now, and at her last words her head, with the damp yellow hair slicked symmetrically back appeared on his level.

"All very well," objected Carlyle. "You can call it courage, but your courage is really built, after all, on a pride of birth. You were bred to that defiant attitude. On my gray days even courage is one of the things that's gray and lifeless."

She was sitting near the edge, hugging her knees and gazing abstractedly at the white moon; he was farther back, crammed like a grotesque god into a niche in the rock.

"I don't want to sound like Pollyanna," she began, "but you haven't grasped me yet. My courage is faith—faith in the eternal resilience of me—that joy'll come back, and hope and spontaneity. And I feel that till it does I've got to keep my lips shut and my chin high, and my eyes wide—not necessarily any silly smiling. Oh, I've been through hell without a whine quite often—and the female hell is deadlier than the male."

"But supposing," suggested Carlyle, "that before joy and hope and all that came back the curtain was drawn on you for good?"

Ardita rose, and going to the wall climbed with some difficulty to the next ledge, another ten or fifteen feet above.

"Why," she called back "then I'd have won!"

He edged out till he could see her.

"Better not dive from there! You'll break your back," he said quickly.

She laughed.

"Not I!"

Slowly she spread her arms and stood there swan-like, radiating a pride in her young perfection that lit a warm glow in Carlyle's heart.

"We're going through the black air with our arms wide and our feet straight out behind like a dolphin's tail, and we're going to think we'll never hit the silver down there till suddenly it'll be all warm round us and full of little kissing, caressing waves."

Then she was in the air, and Carlyle involuntarily held his breath. He had not realized that the dive was nearly forty feet. It seemed an eternity before he heard the swift compact sound as she reached the sea.

And it was with his glad sigh of relief when her light watery laughter curled up the side of the cliff and into his anxious ears that he knew he loved her.

VI

Time, having no axe to grind, showered down upon them three days of afternoons. When the sun cleared the port-hole of Ardita's cabin an hour after dawn she rose cheerily, donned her bathing-suit, and went up on deck. The negroes would leave their work when they saw her, and crowd, chuckling and chattering, to the rail as she floated, an agile minnow, on and under the surface of the clear water. Again in the cool of the afternoon she would swim—and loll and smoke with Carlyle upon the cliff; or else they would lie on their sides in the sands of the southern beach, talking little, but watching the day fade colorfully and tragically into the infinite langour of a tropical evening.

And with the long, sunny hours Ardita's idea of the episode as incidental, madcap, a sprig of romance in a desert of reality, gradually left her. She dreaded the time when he would strike off southward; she dreaded all the eventualities that presented themselves to her; thoughts were suddenly troublesome and decisions odious. Had prayers found place in the pagan rituals of her soul she would have asked of life only to be unmolested for a while, lazily acquiescent to the ready, naïf flow of Carlyle's ideas, his vivid boyish imagination, and the vein of monomania that seemed to run crosswise through his temperament and colored his every action.

But this is not a story of two on an island, nor concerned primarily with love bred of isolation. It is merely the presentation of two personalities, and its idyllic setting among the palms of the Gulf Stream is quite incidental. Most of us are content to exist and breed and fight for the right to do both, and the dominant idea, the foredoomed attest to control one's destiny, is reserved for the fortunate or unfortunate few. To me the interesting thing about Ardita is the courage that will tarnish with her beauty and youth.

"Take me with you," she said late one night as they sat lazily in the grass under the shadowy spreading palms. The negroes had brought ashore their musical instruments, and the sound of weird ragtime was drifting softly over on the warm breath of the night. "I'd love to reappear in ten years, as a fabulously wealthy high-caste Indian lady," she continued.

Carlyle looked at her quickly.

"You can, you know."

She laughed.

"Is it a proposal of marriage? Extra! Ardita Farnam becomes pirate's bride. Society girl kidnapped by ragtime bank robber."

"It wasn't a bank."

"What was it? Why won't you tell me?"

"I don't want to break down your illusions."

"My dear man, I have no illusions about you."

"I mean your illusions about yourself."

She looked up in surprise.

"About myself! What on earth have I got to do with whatever stray felonies you've committed?"

"That remains to be seen."

She reached over and patted his hand.

"Dear Mr. Curtis Carlyle," she said softly, "are you in love with me?"

"As if it mattered."

"But it does—because I think I'm in love with you."

He looked at her ironically.

"Thus swelling your January total to half a dozen," he suggested. "Suppose I call your bluff and ask you to come to India with me?"

"Shall I?"

He shrugged his shoulders.

"We can get married in Callao."

"What sort of life can you offer me? I don't mean that unkindly, but seriously; what would become of me if the people who want that twenty-thousand-dollar reward ever catch up with you?"

"I thought you weren't afraid."

"I never am—but I won't throw my life away just to show one man I'm not."

"I wish you'd been poor. Just a little poor girl dreaming over a fence in a warm cow country."

"Wouldn't it have been nice?"

"I'd have enjoyed astonishing you—watching your eyes open on things. If you only wanted things! Don't you see?"

"I know—like girls who stare into the windows of jewelry-stores."

"Yes—and want the big oblong watch that's platinum and has diamonds all round the edge. Only you'd decide it was too expensive and choose one of white gold for a hundred dollar. Then I'd say: 'Expensive? I should say not!' And we'd go into the store and pretty soon the platinum one would be gleaming on your wrist."

"That sounds so nice and vulgar—and fun, doesn't it?" murmured Ardita.

"Doesn't it? Can't you see us travelling round and spending money right and left, and being worshipped by bell-boys and waiters? Oh, blessed are the simple rich for they inherit the earth!"

"I honestly wish we were that way."

"I love you, Ardita," he said gently.

Her face lost its childish look for moment and became oddly grave.

"I love to be with you," she said, "more than with any man I've ever met. And I like your looks and your dark old hair, and the way you go over the side of the rail when we come ashore. In fact, Curtis Carlyle, I like all the things you do when you're perfectly natural. I think you've got nerve and you know how I feel about that. Sometimes when you're around I've been tempted to kiss you suddenly and tell you that you were just an idealistic boy with a lot of caste nonsense in his head. Perhaps if I were just a little bit older and a little more bored I'd go with you. As it is, I think I'll go back and marry—that other man."

Over across the silver lake the figures of the negroes writhed and squirmed in the moonlight like acrobats who, having been too long inactive, must go through their tacks from sheer surplus energy. In single file they marched, weaving in concentric circles, now with their heads thrown back, now bent over their instruments like piping fauns. And from trombone and saxaphone ceaselessly whined a blended melody, sometimes riotous and jubilant, sometimes haunting and plaintive as a death-dance from the Congo's heart.

"Let's dance," cried Ardita. "I can't sit still with that perfect jazz going on."

Taking her hand he led her out into a broad stretch of hard sandy soil that the moon flooded with great splendor. They floated out like drifting moths under the rich hazy light, and as the fantastic symphony wept and exulted and wavered and despaired Ardita's last sense of reality dropped away, and she abandoned her imagination to the dreamy summer scents of tropical flowers and the infinite starry spaces overhead, feeling that if she opened her eyes it would be to find herself dancing with a ghost in a land created by her own fancy.

"This is what I should call an exclusive private dance," he whispered.

"I feel quite mad—but delightfully mad!"

"We're enchanted. The shades of unnumbered generations of cannibals are watching us from high up on the side of the cliff there."

"And I'll bet the cannibal women are saying that we dance too close, and that it was immodest of me to come without my nose-ring."

They both laughed softly—and then their laughter died as over across the lake they heard the trombones stop in the middle of a bar, and the saxaphones give a startled moan and fade out.

"What's the matter?" called Carlyle.

After a moment's silence they made out the dark figure of a man rounding the silver lake at a run. As he came closer they saw it was Babe in a state of unusual excitement. He drew up before them and gasped out his news in a breath.

"Ship stan'in' off sho' 'bout half a mile suh. Mose, he uz on watch, he say look's if she's done ancho'd."

"A ship—what kind of a ship?" demanded Carlyle anxiously.

Dismay was in his voice, and Ardita's heart gave a sudden wrench as she saw his whole face suddenly droop.

"He say he don't know, suh."

"Are they landing a boat?"

"No, suh."

"We'll go up," said Carlyle.

They ascended the hill in silence, Ardita's hand still resting in Carlyle's as it had when they finished dancing. She felt it clinch nervously from time to time as though he were unaware of the contact, but though he hurt her she made no attempt to remove it. It seemed an hour's climb before they reached the top and crept cautiously across the silhouetted plateau to the edge of the cliff. After one short look Carlyle involuntarily gave a little cry. It was a revenue boat with six-inch guns mounted fore and aft.

"They know!" he said with a short intake of breath. "They know! They picked up the trail somewhere."

"Are you sure they know about the channel? They may be only standing by to take a look at the island in the morning. From where they are they couldn't see the opening in the cliff."

"They could with field-glasses," he said hopelessly. He looked at his wrist-watch. "It's nearly two now. They won't do anything until dawn, that's certain. Of course there's always the faint possibility that they're waiting for some other ship to join; or for a coaler."

"I suppose we may as well stay right here."

The hour passed and they lay there side by side, very silently, their chins in their hands like dreaming children. In back of them squatted the negroes, patient, resigned, acquiescent, announcing now and then with sonorous snores that not even the presence of danger could subdue their unconquerable African craving for sleep.

Just before five o'clock Babe approached Carlyle. There were half a dozen rifles aboard the Narcissus he said. Had it been decided to offer no resistance?

A pretty good fight might be made, he thought, if they worked out some plan.

Carlyle laughed and shook his head.

"That isn't a Spic army out there, Babe. That's a revenue boat. It'd be like a bow and arrow trying to fight a machine-gun. If you want to bury those bags somewhere and take a chance on recovering them later, go on and do it. But it won't work—they'd dig this island over from one end to the other. It's a lost battle all round, Babe."

Babe inclined his head silently and turned away, and Carlyle's voice was husky as he turned to Ardita.

"There's the best friend I ever had. He'd die for me, and be proud to, if I'd let him."

"You've given up?"

"I've no choice. Of course there's always one way out—the sure way—but that can wait. I wouldn't miss my trial for anything—it'll be an interesting experiment in notoriety. 'Miss Farnam testifies that the pirate's attitude to her was at all times that of a gentleman.'"

"Don't!" she said. "I'm awfully sorry."

When the color faded from the sky and lustreless blue changed to leaden gray a commotion was visible on the ship's deck, and they made out a group of officers clad in white duck, gathered near the rail. They had field-glasses in their hands and were attentively examining the islet.

"It's all up," said Carlyle grimly.

"Damn," whispered Ardita. She felt tears gathering in her eyes "We'll go back to the yacht," he said. "I prefer that to being hunted out up here like a 'possum."

Leaving the plateau they descended the hill, and reaching the lake were rowed out to the yacht by the silent negroes. Then, pale and weary, they sank into the settees and waited.

Half an hour later in the dim gray light the nose of the revenue boat appeared in the channel and stopped, evidently fearing that the bay might be too shallow. From the peaceful look of the yacht, the man and the girl in the settees, and the negroes lounging curiously against the rail, they evidently judged that there would be no resistance, for two boats were lowered casually over the side, one containing an officer and six bluejackets, and the other, four rowers and in the stern two gray-haired men in yachting flannels. Ardita and Carlyle stood up, and half unconsciously started toward each other.

Then he paused and putting his hand suddenly into his pocket he pulled out a round, glittering object and held it out to her.

"What is it?" she asked wonderingly.

"I'm not positive, but I think from the Russian inscription inside that it's your promised bracelet."

"Where—where on earth——"

"It came out of one of those bags. You see, Curtis Carlyle and his Six Black Buddies, in the middle of their performance in the tea-room of the hotel at Palm Beach, suddenly changed their instruments for automatics and held up the crowd. I took this bracelet from a pretty, overrouged woman with red hair."

Ardita frowned and then smiled.

"So that's what you did! You *have* got nerve!"

He bowed.

"A well-known bourgeois quality," he said.

And then dawn slanted dynamically across the deck and flung the shadows reeling into gray corners. The dew rose and turned to golden mist, thin as a dream, enveloping them until they seemed gossamer relics of the late night, infinitely transient and already fading. For a moment sea and sky were breathless, and dawn held a pink hand over the young mouth of life—then from out in the lake came the complaint of a rowboat and the swish of oars.

Suddenly against the golden furnace low in the east their two graceful figures melted into one, and he was kissing her spoiled young mouth.

"It's a sort of glory," he murmured after a second.

She smiled up at him.

"Happy, are you?"

Her sigh was a benediction—an ecstatic surety that she was youth and beauty now as much as she would ever know. For another instant life was radiant and time a phantom and their strength eternal—then there was a bumping, scraping sound as the rowboat scraped alongside.

Up the ladder scrambled the two gray-haired men, the officer and two of the sailors with their hands on their revolvers. Mr. Farnam folded his arms and stood looking at his niece.

"So," he said nodding his head slowly.

With a sigh her arms unwound from Carlyle's neck, and her eyes, transfigured and far away, fell upon the boarding party. Her uncle saw her upper lip slowly swell into that arrogant pout he knew so well.

"So," he repeated savagely. "So this is your idea of—of romance. A runaway affair, with a high-seas pirate."

Ardita glanced at him carelessly.

"What an old fool you are!" she said quietly.

"Is that the best you can say for yourself?"

"No," she said as if considering. "No, there's something else. There's that well-known phrase with which I have ended most of our conversations for the past few years—'Shut up!'"

And with that she turned, included the two old men, the officer, and the two sailors in a curt glance of contempt, and walked proudly down the companionway.

But had she waited an instant longer she would have heard a sound from her uncle quite unfamiliar in most of their interviews. He gave vent to a whole-hearted amused chuckle, in which the second old man joined.

The latter turned briskly to Carlyle, who had been regarding this scene with an air of cryptic amusement.

"Well Toby," he said genially, "you incurable, hare-brained romantic chaser of rainbows, did you find that she was the person you wanted?"

Carlyle smiled confidently.

"Why—naturally," he said "I've been perfectly sure ever since I first heard tell of her wild career. That'd why I had Babe send up the rocket last night."

"I'm glad you did," said Colonel Moreland gravely. "We've been keeping pretty close to you in case you should have trouble with those six strange niggers. And we hoped we'd find you two in some such compromising position," he sighed. "Well, set a crank to catch a crank!"

"Your father and I sat up all night hoping for the best—or perhaps it's the worst. Lord knows you're welcome to her, my boy. She's run me crazy. Did you give her the Russian bracelet my detective got from that Mimi woman?"

Carlyle nodded.

"Sh!" he said. "She's coming on deck."

Ardita appeared at the head of the companionway and gave a quick involuntary glance at Carlyle's wrists. A puzzled look passed across her face. Back aft the negroes had begun to sing, and the cool lake, fresh with dawn, echoed serenely to their low voices.

"Ardita," said Carlyle unsteadily.

She swayed a step toward him.

"Ardita," he repeated breathlessly, "I've got to tell you the— the truth. It was all a plant, Ardita. My name isn't Carlyle. It's Moreland, Toby Moreland. The story was invented, Ardita, invented out of thin Florida air."

She stared at him, bewildered, amazement, disbelief, and anger flowing in quick waves across her face. The three men held their breaths. Moreland, Senior, took a step toward her; Mr. Farnam's mouth dropped a little open as he waited, panic-stricken, for the expected crash.

But it did not come. Ardita's face became suddenly radiant, and with a little laugh she went swiftly to young Moreland and looked up at him without a trace of wrath in her gray eyes.

"Will you swear," she said quietly "That it was entirely a product of your own brain?"

"I swear," said young Moreland eagerly.

She drew his head down and kissed him gently.

"What an imagination!" she said softly and almost enviously. "I want you to lie to me just as sweetly as you know how for the rest of my life."

The negroes' voices floated drowsily back, mingled in an air that she had heard them singing before.

> "Time is a thief;
> Gladness and grief
> Cling to the leaf
>   As it yellows——"

"What was in the bags?" she asked softly.

"Florida mud," he answered. "That was one of the two true things I told you."

"Perhaps I can guess the other one," she said; and reaching up on her tiptoes she kissed him softly in the illustration.

"O RUSSET WITCH!"

First published in
Metropolitan Magazine, February, 1921

I

Merlin Grainger was employed by the Moonlight Quill Bookshop, which you may have visited, just around the corner from the Ritz-Carlton on Forty-seventh Street. The Moonlight Quill is, or rather was, a very romantic little store, considered radical and admitted dark. It was spotted interiorly with red and orange posters of breathless exotic intent, and lit no less by the shiny reflecting bindings of special editions than by the great squat lamp of crimson satin that, lighted through all the day, swung overhead. It was truly a mellow bookshop. The words "Moonlight Quill" were worked over the door in a sort of serpentine embroidery. The windows seemed always full of something that had passed the literary censors with little to spare; volumes with covers of deep orange which offer their titles on little white paper squares. And over all there was the smell of the musk, which the clever, inscrutable Mr. Moonlight Quill ordered to be sprinkled about—the smell half of a curiosity shop in Dickens' London and half of a coffee-house on the warm shores of the Bosphorus.

From nine until five-thirty Merlin Grainger asked bored old ladies in black and young men with dark circles under their eyes if they "cared for this fellow" or were interested in first editions. Did they buy novels with Arabs on the cover, or books which gave Shakespeare's newest sonnets as dictated psychically to Miss Sutton of South Dakota? he sniffed. As a matter of fact, his own taste ran to these latter, but as an employee at the Moonlight Quill he assumed for the working day the attitude of a disillusioned connoisseur.

After he had crawled over the window display to pull down the front shade at five-thirty every afternoon, and said good-bye to the mysterious Mr. Moonlight Quill and the lady clerk, Miss McCracken, and the lady stenographer, Miss Masters, he went home to the girl, Caroline. He did not eat supper with Caroline. It is unbelievable that Caroline would have considered eating off his bureau with the collar buttons dangerously near the cottage cheese, and the ends of Merlin's necktie just missing his glass of milk—he had never asked her to eat with him. He ate alone. He went into Braegdort's delicatessen on Sixth Avenue and bought a box of crackers, a tube of anchovy paste, and some oranges, or else a little jar of sausages and some potato salad and a bottled soft drink, and with these in a brown package he went to his room at Fifty-something West Fifty-eighth Street and ate his supper and saw Caroline.

Caroline was a very young and gay person who lived with some older lady and was possibly nineteen. She was like a ghost in that she never existed until evening. She sprang into life when the lights went on in her apartment at about six, and she disappeared, at the latest, about midnight. Her apartment was a nice one, in a nice building with a white stone front, opposite the south side of Central Park. The back of her apartment faced the single window of the single room occupied by the single Mr. Grainger.

He called her Caroline because there was a picture that looked like her on the jacket of a book of that name down at the Moonlight Quill.

Now, Merlin Grainger was a thin young man of twenty-five, with dark hair and no mustache or beard or anything like that, but Caroline was dazzling and light, with a shimmering morass of russet waves to take the place of hair, and the sort of features that remind you of kisses—the sort of features you thought belonged to your first love, but know, when you come across an old picture, didn't. She dressed in pink or blue usually, but of late she had sometimes put on a slender black gown that was evidently her especial pride, for whenever she wore it she would stand regarding a certain place on the wall, which Merlin thought must be a mirror. She sat usually in the profile chair near the window, but sometimes honored the *chaise longue* by the lamp, and often she leaned 'way back and smoked a cigarette with posturings of her arms and hands that Merlin considered very graceful.

At another time she had come to the window and stood in it magnificently, and looked out because the moon had lost its way and was dripping the strangest and most transforming brilliance into the areaway between, turning the motif of ash-cans and clothes-lines into a vivid impressionism of silver casks and gigantic gossamer cobwebs. Merlin was sitting in plain sight, eating cottage cheese with sugar and milk on it; and so quickly did he reach out for the window cord that he tipped the cottage cheese into his lap with his free hand—and the milk was cold and the sugar made spots on his trousers, and he was sure that she had seen him after all.

Sometimes there were callers—men in dinner coats, who stood and bowed, hat in hand and coat on arm, as they talked to Caroline; then bowed some more and followed her out of the light, obviously bound for a play or for a dance. Other young men came and sat and smoked cigarettes, and seemed trying to tell Caroline something—she sitting either in the profile chair and watching them with eager intentness or else in the *chaise longue* by the lamp, looking very lovely and youthfully inscrutable indeed.

Merlin enjoyed these calls. Of some of the men he approved. Others won only his grudging toleration, one or two he loathed—especially the most frequent caller, a man with black hair and a black goatee and a pitch-dark soul, who seemed to Merlin vaguely familiar, but whom he was never quite able to recognize.

Now, Merlin's whole life was not "bound up with this romance he had constructed"; it was not "the happiest hour of his day." He never arrived in time to rescue Caroline from "clutches"; nor did he even marry her. A much stranger thing happened than any of these, and it is this strange thing that will presently be set down here. It began one October afternoon when she walked briskly into the mellow interior of the Moonlight Quill.

It was a dark afternoon, threatening rain and the end of the world, and done in that particularly gloomy gray in which only New York afternoons indulge. A breeze was crying down the streets, whisking along battered newspapers and pieces of things, and little lights were pricking out all the windows—it was so desolate that one was sorry for the tops of sky-scrapers lost up there in the dark green and gray heaven, and felt that now surely the farce was to close, and presently all the buildings would collapse like card houses, and pile up in a dusty, sardonic heap upon all the millions who presumed to wind in and out of them.

At least these were the sort of musings that lay heavily upon the soul of Merlin Grainger, as he stood by the window putting a dozen books back in a row after a cyclonic visit by a lady with ermine trimmings. He looked out of the window full of the most distressing thoughts—of the early novels of H. G. Wells, of the book of Genesis, of how Thomas Edison had said that in thirty years there would be no dwelling-houses upon the island, but only a vast and turbulent bazaar; and then he set the last book right side up, turned—and Caroline walked coolly into the shop.

She was dressed in a jaunty but conventional walking costume—he remembered this when he thought about it later. Her skirt was plaid, pleated like a concertina; her jacket was a soft but brisk tan; her shoes and spats were brown and her hat, small and trim, completed her like the top of a very expensive and beautifully filled candy box.

Merlin, breathless and startled, advanced nervously toward her.

"Good-afternoon—" he said, and then stopped—why, he did not know, except that it came to him that something very portentous in his life was about to occur, and that it would need no furbishing but silence, and the proper amount of expectant attention. And in that minute before the thing began to happen he had the sense of a breathless second hanging suspended in time: he saw through the glass partition that bounded off the little office the malevolent conical head of his employer, Mr. Moonlight Quill, bent over his correspondence. He saw Miss McCracken and Miss Masters as two patches of hair drooping over piles of paper; he saw the crimson lamp overhead, and noticed with a touch of pleasure how really pleasant and romantic it made the book-store seem.

Then the thing happened, or rather it began to happen. Caroline picked up a volume of poems lying loose upon a pile, fingered it absently with her slender white hand, and suddenly, with an easy gesture, tossed it upward toward the ceiling where it disappeared in the crimson lamp and lodged there, seen through the illuminated silk as a dark, bulging rectangle. This pleased her—she broke into young, contagious laughter, in which Merlin found himself presently joining.

"It stayed up!" she cried merrily. "It stayed up, didn't it?" To both of them this seemed the height of brilliant absurdity. Their laughter mingled, filled the bookshop, and Merlin was glad to find that her voice was rich and full of sorcery.

"Try another," he found himself suggesting—"try a red one."

At this her laughter increased, and she had to rest her hands upon the stack to steady herself.

"Try another," she managed to articulate between spasms of mirth. "Oh, golly, try another!"

"Try two."

"Yes, try two. Oh, I'll choke if I don't stop laughing.

Here it goes."

Suiting her action to the word, she picked up a red book and sent it in a gentle hyperbola toward the ceiling, where it sank into the lamp beside the first. It was a few minutes before either of them could do more than rock back and forth in helpless glee; but then by mutual agreement they took up the sport anew, this time in unison. Merlin seized a large, specially bound French classic and whirled it upward. Applauding his own accuracy, he took a best-seller in one hand and a book on barnacles in the other, and waited breathlessly while she made her shot. Then the business waxed fast and furious—sometimes they alternated, and, watching, he found how supple she was in every movement; sometimes one of them made shot after shot, picking up the nearest book, sending it off, merely taking time to follow it with a glance before reaching for another. Within three minutes they had cleared a little place on the table, and the lamp of crimson satin was so bulging with books that it was near breaking.

"Silly game, basket-ball," she cried scornfully as a book left her hand. "High-school girls play it in hideous bloomers."

"Idiotic," he agreed.

She paused in the act of tossing a book, and replaced it suddenly in its position on the table.

"I think we've got room to sit down now," she said gravely.

They had; they had cleared an ample space for two. With a faint touch of nervousness Merlin glanced toward Mr. Moonlight Quill's glass partition, but the three heads were still bent earnestly over their work, and it was evident that they had not seen what had gone on in the shop. So when Caroline put her hands on the table and hoisted herself up Merlin calmly imitated her, and they sat side by side looking very earnestly at each other.

"I had to see you," she began, with a rather pathetic expression in her brown eyes.

"I know."

"It was that last time," she continued, her voice trembling

a little, though she tried to keep it steady. "I was frightened. I don't like you to eat off the dresser. I'm so afraid you'll—you'll swallow a collar button."

"I did once—almost," he confessed reluctantly, "but it's not so easy, you know. I mean you can swallow the flat part easy enough or else the other part—that is, separately—but for a whole collar button you'd have to have a specially made throat." He was astonishing himself by the debonnaire appropriateness of his remarks. Words seemed for the first time in his life to run at him shrieking to be used, gathering themselves into carefully arranged squads and platoons, and being presented to him by punctilious adjutants of paragraphs.

"That's what scared me," she said. "I knew you had to have a specially made throat—and I knew, at least I felt sure, that you didn't have one."

He nodded frankly.

"I haven't. It costs money to have one—more money unfortunately than I possess."

He felt no shame in saying this—rather a delight in making the admission—he knew that nothing he could say or do would be beyond her comprehension; least of all his poverty, and the practical impossibility of ever extricating himself from it.

Caroline looked down at her wrist watch, and with a little cry slid from the table to her feet.

"It's after five," she cried. "I didn't realize. I have to be at the Ritz at five-thirty. Let's hurry and get this done. I've got a bet on it."

With one accord they set to work. Caroline began the matter by seizing a book on insects and sending it whizzing, and finally crashing through the glass partition that housed Mr. Moonlight Quill. The proprietor glanced up with a wild look, brushed a few pieces of glass from his desk, and went on with his letters. Miss McCracken gave no sign of having heard—only Miss Masters started and gave a little frightened scream before she bent to her task again.

But to Merlin and Caroline it didn't matter. In a perfect orgy of energy they were hurling book after book in all directions until sometimes three or four were in the air at once, smashing against shelves, cracking the glass of pictures on the walls, falling in bruised and torn heaps upon the floor. It was fortunate that no customers happened to come in, for it is certain they would never have come in again—the noise was too tremendous, a noise of smashing and ripping and tearing, mixed now and then with the tinkling of glass, the quick breathing of the two throwers, and the intermittent outbursts of laughter to which both of them periodically surrendered.

At five-thirty Caroline tossed a last book at the lamp, and gave the final impetus to the load it carried. The weakened silk tore and dropped its cargo in one vast splattering of white and color to the already littered floor. Then with a sigh of relief she turned to Merlin and held out her hand.

"Good-by," she said simply.

"Are you going?" He knew she was. His question was simply a lingering wile to detain her and extract for another moment that dazzling essence of light he drew from her presence, to continue his enormous satisfaction in her features, which were like kisses and, he thought, like the features of a girl he had known back in 1910. For a minute he pressed the softness of her hand— then she smiled and withdrew it and, before he could spring to open the door, she had done it herself and was gone out into the turbid and ominous twilight that brooded narrowly over Forty-seventh Street.

I would like to tell you how Merlin, having seen how beauty regards the wisdom of the years, walked into the little partition of Mr. Moonlight Quill and gave up his job then and there; thence issuing out into the street a much finer and nobler and increasingly ironic man. But the truth is much more commonplace. Merlin Grainger stood up and surveyed the wreck of the bookshop, the ruined volumes, the torn silk remnants of the once beautiful crimson lamp, the crystalline sprinkling of broken glass which lay in iridescent dust over the whole interior—and then he went to a corner where a broom was kept and began cleaning up and rearranging and, as far as he was able, restoring the shop to its former condition. He found that, though some few of the books were uninjured, most of them had suffered in varying extents. The backs were off some, the pages were torn from others, still others were just slightly cracked in the front, which, as all careless book returners know, makes a book unsalable, and therefore second-hand.

Nevertheless by six o'clock he had done much to repair the damage. He had returned the books to their original places, swept the floor, and put new lights in the sockets overhead. The red shade itself was ruined beyond redemption, and Merlin thought in some trepidation that the money to replace it might have to come out of his salary. At six, therefore, having done the best he could, he crawled over the front window display to pull down the blind. As he was treading delicately back, he saw Mr. Moonlight Quill rise from his desk, put on his overcoat and hat, and emerge into the shop. He nodded mysteriously at Merlin and went toward the door. With his hand on the knob he paused, turned around, and in a voice curiously compounded of ferocity and uncertainty, he said:

"If that girl comes in here again, you tell her to behave."

With that he opened the door, drowning Merlin's meek "Yessir" in its creak, and went out.

Merlin stood there for a moment, deciding wisely not to worry about what was for the present only a possible futurity, and then he went into the back of the shop and invited Miss Masters to have supper with him at Pulpat's French Restaurant, where one could still obtain red wine at dinner, despite the Great Federal Government. Miss Masters accepted.

"Wine makes me feel all tingly," she said.

Merlin laughed inwardly as he compared her to Caroline, or rather as he didn't compare her. There was no comparison.

II

Mr. Moonlight Quill, mysterious, exotic, and oriental in temperament was, nevertheless, a man of decision. And it was with decision that he approached the problem of his wrecked shop. Unless he should make an outlay equal to the original cost of his entire stock—a step which for certain private reasons he did not wish to take—it would be impossible for him to continue in business with the Moonlight Quill as before. There was but one thing to do. He promptly turned his establishment from an up-to-the-minute book-store into a second-hand bookshop. The damaged books were marked down from twenty-five to fifty per cent, the name over the door whose serpentine embroidery had once shone so insolently bright, was allowed to grow dim and take on the indescribably vague color of old paint, and, having a strong penchant for ceremonial, the proprietor even went so far as to buy two skull-caps of shoddy red felt, one for himself and one for his clerk, Merlin Grainger. Moreover, he let his goatee grow until it resembled the tail-feathers of an ancient sparrow and substituted for a once dapper business suit a reverence-inspiring affair of shiny alpaca.

In fact, within a year after Caroline's catastrophic visit to the bookshop the only thing in it that preserved any semblance of being up to date was Miss Masters. Miss McCracken had followed in the footsteps of Mr. Moonlight Quill and become an intolerable dowd.

For Merlin too, from a feeling compounded of loyalty and listlessness, had let his exterior take on the semblance of a deserted garden. He accepted the red felt skull-cap as a symbol of his decay. Always a young man known as a "pusher," he had been, since the day of his graduation from the manual training department of a New York High School, an inveterate brusher of clothes, hair, teeth, and even eyebrows, and had learned the value of laying all his clean socks toe upon toe and heel upon heel in a certain drawer of his bureau, which would be known as the sock drawer.

These things, he felt, had won him his place in the greatest splendor of the Moonlight Quill. It was due to them that he was not still making "chests useful for keeping things," as he was taught with breathless practicality in High School, and selling them to whoever had use of such chests—possibly undertakers. Nevertheless when the progressive Moonlight Quill became the retrogressive Moonlight Quill he preferred to sink with it, and so took to letting his suits gather undisturbed the wispy burdens of the air and to throwing his socks indiscriminately into the shirt drawer, the underwear drawer, and even into no drawer at all. It was not uncommon in his new carelessness to let many of his clean clothes go directly back to the laundry without having ever been worn, a common eccentricity of impoverished bachelors. And this in the face of his favorite magazines, which at that time were fairly staggering with articles by successful authors against the frightful impudence of the condemned poor, such as the buying of wearable shirts and nice cuts of meat, and the fact that they preferred good investments in personal jewelry to respectable ones in four per cent saving-banks.

It was indeed a strange state of affairs and a sorry one for many worthy and God-fearing men. For the first time in the history of the Republic almost any negro north of Georgia could change a one-dollar bill. But as at that time the cent was rapidly approaching the purchasing power of the Chinese ubu and was only a thing you got back occasionally after paying for a soft drink, and could use merely in getting your correct weight, this was perhaps not so strange a phenomenon as it at first seems. It was too curious a state of things, however, for Merlin Grainger to take the step that he did take—the hazardous, almost involuntary step of proposing to Miss Masters. Stranger still that she accepted him.

It was at Pulpat's on Saturday night and over a $1.75 bottle of water diluted with *vin ordinaire* that the proposal occurred.

"Wine makes me feel all tingly, doesn't it you?" chattered

Miss Masters gaily.

"Yes," answered Merlin absently; and then, after a long and pregnant pause: "Miss Masters—Olive—I want to say something to you if you'll listen to me."

The tingliness of Miss Masters (who knew what was coming) increased until it seemed that she would shortly be electrocuted by her own nervous reactions. But her "Yes, Merlin," came without a sign or flicker of interior disturbance. Merlin swallowed a stray bit of air that he found in his mouth.

"I have no fortune," he said with the manner of making an announcement. "I have no fortune at all."

Their eyes met, locked, became wistful, and dreamy and beautiful.

"Olive," he told her, "I love you."

"I love you too, Merlin," she answered simply. "Shall we have another bottle of wine?"

"Yes," he cried, his heart beating at a great rate. "Do you mean—"

"To drink to our engagement," she interrupted bravely. "May it be a short one!"

"No!" he almost shouted, bringing his fist fiercely down upon the table. "May it last forever!"

"What?"

"I mean—oh, I see what you mean. You're right. May it be a short one." He laughed and added, "My error."

After the wine arrived they discussed the matter thoroughly.

"We'll have to take a small apartment at first," he said, "and I believe, yes, by golly, I know there's a small one in the house where I live, a big room and a sort of a dressing-room-kitchenette and the use of a bath on the same floor."

She clapped her hands happily, and he thought how pretty she was really, that is, the upper part of her face—from the bridge of the nose down she was somewhat out of true. She continued enthusiastically:

"And as soon as we can afford it we'll take a real swell

apartment, with an elevator and a telephone girl."

"And after that a place in the country—and a car."

"I can't imagine nothing more fun. Can you?"

Merlin fell silent a moment. He was thinking that he would have to give up his room, the fourth floor rear. Yet it mattered very little now. During the past year and a half—in fact, from the very date of Caroline's visit to the Moonlight Quill—he had never seen her. For a week after that visit her lights had failed to go on—darkness brooded out into the areaway, seemed to grope blindly in at his expectant, uncurtained window. Then the lights had appeared at last, and instead of Caroline and her callers they showed a stodgy family—a little man with a bristly mustache and a full-bosomed woman who spent her evenings patting her hips and rearranging bric-à-brac. After two days of them Merlin had callously pulled down his shade.

No, Merlin could think of nothing more fun than rising in the world with Olive. There would be a cottage in a suburb, a cottage painted blue, just one class below the sort of cottages that are of white stucco with a green roof. In the grass around the cottage would be rusty trowels and a broken green bench and a baby-carriage with a wicker body that sagged to the left. And around the grass and the baby-carriage and the cottage itself, around his whole world there would be the arms of Olive, a little stouter, the arms of her neo-Olivian period, when, as she walked, her cheeks would tremble up and down ever so slightly from too much face-massaging. He could hear her voice now, two spoons' length away:

"I knew you were going to say this to-night, Merlin. I could see—"

She could see. Ah—suddenly he wondered how much she could see. Could she see that the girl who had come in with a party of three men and sat down at the next table was Caroline? Ah, could she see that? Could she see that the men brought with them liquor far more potent than Pulpat's red ink condensed threefold? . . .

Merlin stared breathlessly, half-hearing through an auditory ether Olive's low, soft monologue, as like a persistent honey-bee she sucked sweetness from her memorable hour. Merlin was listening to the clinking of ice and the fine laughter of all four at some pleasantry—and that laughter of Caroline's that he knew so well stirred him, lifted him, called his heart imperiously over to her table, whither it obediently went. He could see her quite plainly, and he fancied that in the last year and a half she had changed, if ever so slightly. Was it the light or were her cheeks a little thinner and her eyes less fresh, if more liquid, than of old? Yet the shadows were still purple in her russet hair; her mouth hinted yet of kisses, as did the profile that came sometimes between his eyes and a row of books, when it was twilight in the bookshop where the crimson lamp presided no more.

And she had been drinking. The threefold flush in her cheeks was compounded of youth and wine and fine cosmetic—that he could tell. She was making great amusement for the young man on her left and the portly person on her right, and even for the old fellow opposite her, for the latter from time to time uttered the shocked and mildly reproachful cackles of another generation. Merlin caught the words of a song she was intermittently singing—

> *"Just snap your fingers at care,*
> *Don't cross the bridge 'til you're there—"*

The portly person filled her glass with chill amber. A waiter after several trips about the table, and many helpless glances at Caroline, who was maintaining a cheerful, futile questionnaire as to the succulence of this dish or that, managed to obtain the semblance of an order and hurried away . . .

Olive was speaking to Merlin—

"When, then?" she asked, her voice faintly shaded with disappointment. He realized that he had just answered no to some question she had asked him.

"Oh, sometime."

"Don't you—care?"

A rather pathetic poignancy in her question brought his eyes back to her.

"As soon as possible, dear," he replied with surprising tenderness. "In two months—in June."

"So soon?" Her delightful excitement quite took her breath away.

"Oh, yes, I think we'd better say June. No use waiting."

Olive began to pretend that two months was really too short a time for her to make preparations. Wasn't he a bad boy! Wasn't he impatient, though! Well, she'd show him he mustn't be too quick with *her*. Indeed he was so sudden she didn't exactly know whether she ought to marry him at all.

"June," he repeated sternly.

Olive sighed and smiled and drank her coffee, her little finger lifted high above the others in true refined fashion. A stray thought came to Merlin that he would like to buy five rings and throw at it.

"By gosh!" he exclaimed aloud. Soon he *would* be putting rings on one of her fingers.

His eyes swung sharply to the right. The party of four had become so riotous that the head-waiter had approached and spoken to them. Caroline was arguing with this head-waiter in a raised voice, a voice so clear and young that it seemed as though the whole restaurant would listen—the whole restaurant except Olive Masters, self-absorbed in her new secret.

"How do you do?" Caroline was saying. "Probably the handsomest head-waiter in captivity. Too much noise? Very unfortunate. Something'll have to be done about it. Gerald"— she addressed the man on her right—"the head-waiter says there's too much noise. Appeals to us to have it stopped. What'll I say?"

"Sh!" remonstrated Gerald, with laughter. "Sh!" and Merlin heard him add in an undertone: "All the bourgeoisie will be aroused. This is where the floorwalkers learn French."

Caroline sat up straight in sudden alertness.

"Where's a floorwalker?" she cried. "Show me a floorwalker." This seemed to amuse the party, for they all, including Caroline, burst into renewed laughter. The head-waiter, after a last conscientious but despairing admonition, became Gallic with his shoulders and retired into the background.

Pulpat's, as every one knows, has the unvarying respectability of the table d'hôte. It is not a gay place in the conventional sense. One comes, drinks the red wine, talks perhaps a little more and a little louder than usual under the low, smoky ceilings, and then goes home. It closes up at nine-thirty, tight as a drum; the policeman is paid off and given an extra bottle of wine for the missis, the coat-room girl hands her tips to the collector, and then darkness crushes the little round tables out of sight and life. But excitement was prepared for Pulpat's this evening—excitement of no mean variety. A girl with russet, purple-shadowed hair mounted to her table-top and began to dance thereon.

"*Sacrè nom de Dieu!* Come down off there!" cried the head-waiter. "Stop that music!"

But the musicians were already playing so loud that they could pretend not to hear his order; having once been young, they played louder and gayer than ever, and Caroline danced with grace and vivacity, her pink, filmy dress swirling about her, her agile arms playing in supple, tenuous gestures along the smoky air.

A group of Frenchmen at a table near by broke into cries of applause, in which other parties joined—in a moment the room was full of clapping and shouting; half the diners were on their feet, crowding up, and on the outskirts the hastily summoned proprietor was giving indistinct vocal evidences of his desire to put an end to this thing as quickly as possible.

" . . . Merlin!" cried Olive, awake, aroused at last; "she's such a wicked girl! Let's get out—now!"

The fascinated Merlin protested feebly that the check was not paid.

"It's all right. Lay five dollars on the table. I despise that girl. I can't *bear* to look at her." She was on her feet now, tagging at Merlin's arm.

Helplessly, listlessly, and then with what amounted to downright unwillingness, Merlin rose, followed Olive dumbly as she picked her way through the delirious clamor, now approaching its height and threatening to become a wild and memorable riot. Submissively he took his coat and stumbled up half a dozen steps into the moist April air outside, his ears still ringing with the sound of light feet on the table and of laughter all about and over the little world of the café. In silence they walked along toward Fifth Avenue and a bus.

It was not until next day that she told him about the wedding—how she had moved the date forward: it was much better that they should be married on the first of May.

III

And married they were, in a somewhat stuffy manner, under the chandelier of the flat where Olive lived with her mother. After marriage came elation, and then, gradually, the growth of weariness. Responsibility descended upon Merlin, the responsibility of making his thirty dollars a week and her twenty suffice to keep them respectably fat and to hide with decent garments the evidence that they were.

It was decided after several weeks of disastrous and well-nigh humiliating experiments with restaurants that they would join the great army of the delicatessen-fed, so he took up his old way of life again, in that he stopped every evening at Braegdort's delicatessen and bought potatoes in salad, ham in slices, and sometimes even stuffed tomatoes in bursts of extravagance.

Then he would trudge homeward, enter the dark hallway, and

climb three rickety flights of stairs covered by an ancient carpet of long obliterated design. The hall had an ancient smell—of the vegetables of 1880, of the furniture polish in vogue when "Adam-and Eve" Bryan ran against William McKinley, of portieres an ounce heavier with dust, from worn-out shoes, and lint from dresses turned long since into patch-work quilts. This smell would pursue him up the stairs, revivified and made poignant at each landing by the aura of contemporary cooking, then, as he began the next flight, diminishing into the odor of the dead routine of dead generations.

Eventually would occur the door of his room, which slipped open with indecent willingness and closed with almost a sniff upon his "Hello, dear! Got a treat for you to-night."

Olive, who always rode home on the bus to "get a morsel of air," would be making the bed and hanging up things. At his call she would come up to him and give him a quick kiss with wide-open eyes, while he held her upright like a ladder, his hands on her two arms, as though she were a thing without equilibrium, and would, once he relinquished hold, fall stiffly backward to the floor. This is the kiss that comes in with the second year of marriage, succeeding the bridegroom kiss (which is rather stagey at best, say those who know about such things, and apt to be copied from passionate movies).

Then came supper, and after that they went out for a walk, up two blocks and through Central Park, or sometimes to a moving picture, which taught them patiently that they were the sort of people for whom life was ordered, and that something very grand and brave and beautiful would soon happen to them if they were docile and obedient to their rightful superiors and kept away from pleasure.

Such was their day for three years. Then change came into their lives: Olive had a baby, and as a result Merlin had a new influx of material resources. In the third week of Olive's confinement, after an hour of nervous rehearsing, he went into the office of Mr. Moonlight Quill and demanded an enormous increase in salary.

"I've been here ten years," he said; "since I was nineteen. I've always tried to do my best in the interests of the business."

Mr. Moonlight Quill said that he would think it over. Next morning he announced, to Merlin's great delight, that he was going to put into effect a project long premeditated—he was going to retire from active work in the bookshop, confining himself to periodic visits and leaving Merlin as manager with a salary of fifty dollars a week and a one-tenth interest in the business. When the old man finished, Merlin's cheeks were glowing and his eyes full of tears. He seized his employer's hand and shook it violently, saying over and over again:

"It's very nice of you, sir. It's very white of you. It's very, very nice of you."

So after ten years of faithful work in the store he had won out at last. Looking back, he saw his own progress toward this hill of elation no longer as a sometimes sordid and always gray decade of worry and failing enthusiasm and failing dreams, years when the moonlight had grown duller in the areaway and the youth had faded out of Olive's face, but as a glorious and triumphant climb over obstacles which he had determinedly surmounted by unconquerable will-power. The optimistic self-delusion that had kept him from misery was seen now in the golden garments of stern resolution. Half a dozen times he had taken steps to leave the Moonlight Quill and soar upward, but through sheer faintheartedness he had stayed on. Strangely enough he now thought that those were times when he had exerted tremendous persistence and had "determined" to fight it out where he was.

At any rate, let us not for this moment begrudge Merlin his new and magnificent view of himself. He had arrived. At thirty he had reached a post of importance. He left the shop that evening fairly radiant, invested every penny in his pocket in the most tremendous feast that Braegdort's delicatessen offered, and staggered homeward with the great news and four gigantic paper bags. The fact that Olive was too sick to eat, that he made himself faintly but unmistakably ill by a struggle with four stuffed tomatoes, and that most of the food deteriorated rapidly in an iceless ice-box: all next day did not mar the occasion. For the first time since the week of his marriage Merlin Grainger lived under a sky of unclouded tranquillity.

The baby boy was christened Arthur, and life became dignified, significant, and, at length, centered. Merlin and Olive resigned themselves to a somewhat secondary place in their own cosmos; but what they lost in personality they regained in a sort of primordial pride. The country house did not come, but a month in an Asbury Park boarding-house each summer filled the gap; and during Merlin's two weeks' holiday this excursion assumed the air of a really merry jaunt—especially when, with the baby asleep in a wide room opening technically on the sea, Merlin strolled with Olive along the thronged board-walk puffing at his cigar and trying to look like twenty thousand a year.

With some alarm at the slowing up of the days and the accelerating of the years, Merlin became thirty one, thirty-two—then almost with a rush arrived at that age which, with all its washing and panning, can only muster a bare handful of the precious stuff of youth: he became thirty-five. And one day on Fifth Avenue he saw Caroline.

It was Sunday, a radiant, flowerful Easter morning and the avenue was a pageant of lilies and cutaways and happy April-colored bonnets. Twelve o'clock: the great churches were letting out their people—St. Simon's, St. Hilda's, the Church of the Epistles, opened their doors like wide mouths until the people pouring forth surely resembled happy laughter as they met and strolled and chattered, or else waved white bouquets at waiting chauffeurs.

In front of the Church of the Epistles stood its twelve vestrymen, carrying out the time-honored custom of giving away Easter eggs full of face-powder to the church-going débutantes of the year. Around them delightedly danced the two thousand miraculously groomed children of the very rich, correctly cute and curled, shining like sparkling little jewels upon their mothers' fingers. Speaks the sentimentalist for the children of the poor? Ah, but the children of the rich, laundered, sweet-smelling, complexioned of the country, and, above all, with soft, in-door voices.

Little Arthur was five, child of the middle class. Undistinguished, unnoticed, with a nose that forever marred what Grecian yearnings his features might have had, he held tightly to his mother's warm, sticky hand, and, with Merlin on his other side, moved upon the home-coming throng. At Fifty-third Street, where there were two churches, the congestion was at its thickest, its richest. Their progress was of necessity retarded to such an extent that even little Arthur had not the slightest difficulty in keeping up. Then it was that Merlin perceived an open landaulet of deepest crimson, with handsome nickel trimmings, glide slowly up to the curb and come to a stop. In it sat Caroline.

She was dressed in black, a tight-fitting gown trimmed with lavender, flowered at the waist with a corsage of orchids. Merlin started and then gazed at her fearfully. For the first time in the eight years since his marriage he was encountering the girl again. But a girl no longer. Her figure was slim as ever— or perhaps not quite, for a certain boyish swagger, a sort of insolent adolescence, had gone the way of the first blooming of her cheeks. But she was beautiful; dignity was there now, and the charming lines of a fortuitous nine-and-twenty; and she sat in the car with such perfect appropriateness and self-possession that it made him breathless to watch her.

Suddenly she smiled—the smile of old, bright as that very Easter and its flowers, mellower than ever—yet somehow with not quite the radiance and infinite promise of that first smile back there in the bookshop nine years before. It was a steelier smile, disillusioned and sad.

But it was soft enough and smile enough to make a pair of

young men in cutaway coats hurry over, to pull their high hats off their wetted, iridescent hair; to bring them, flustered and bowing, to the edge of her landaulet, where her lavender gloves gently touched their gray ones. And these two were presently joined by another, and then two more, until there was a rapidly swelling crowd around the landaulet. Merlin would hear a young man beside him say to his perhaps well-favored companion:

"If you'll just pardon me a moment, there's some one I *have* to speak to. Walk right ahead. I'll catch up."

Within three minutes every inch of the landaulet, front, back, and side, was occupied by a man—a man trying to construct a sentence clever enough to find its way to Caroline through the stream of conversation. Luckily for Merlin a portion of little Arthur's clothing had chosen the opportunity to threaten a collapse, and Olive had hurriedly rushed him over against a building for some extemporaneous repair work, so Merlin was able to watch, unhindered, the salon in the street.

The crowd swelled. A row formed in back of the first, two more behind that. In the midst, an orchid rising from a black bouquet, sat Caroline enthroned in her obliterated car, nodding and crying salutations and smiling with such true happiness that, of a sudden, a new relay of gentlemen had left their wives and consorts and were striding toward her.

The crowd, now phalanx deep, began to be augmented by the merely curious; men of all ages who could not possibly have known Caroline jostled over and melted into the circle of ever-increasing diameter, until the lady in lavender was the centre of a vast impromptu auditorium.

All about her were faces—clean-shaven, bewhiskered, old, young, ageless, and now, here and there, a woman. The mass was rapidly spreading to the opposite curb, and, as St. Anthony's around the corner let out its box-holders, it overflowed to the sidewalk and crushed up against the iron picket-fence of a millionaire across the street. The motors speeding along the avenue were compelled to stop, and in a jiffy were piled three, five, and six deep at the edge of the crowd; auto-busses, top-heavy turtles of traffic, plunged into the jam, their passengers crowding to the edges of the roofs in wild excitement and peering down into the centre of the mass, which presently could hardly be seen from the mass's edge.

The crush had become terrific. No fashionable audience at a Yale-Princeton football game, no damp mob at a world's series, could be compared with the panoply that talked, stared, laughed, and honked about the lady in black and lavender. It was stupendous; it was terrible. A quarter mile down the block a half-frantic policeman called his precinct; on the same corner a frightened civilian crashed in the glass of a fire-alarm and sent in a wild paean for all the fire-engines of the city; up in an apartment high in one of the tall buildings a hysterical old maid telephoned in turn for the prohibition enforcement agent; the special deputies on Bolshevism, and the maternity ward of Bellevue Hospital.

The noise increased. The first fire-engine arrived, filling the Sunday air with smoke, clanging and crying a brazen, metallic message down the high, resounding walls. In the notion that some terrible calamity had overtaken the city, two excited deacons ordered special services immediately and set tolling the great bells of St. Hilda's and St. Anthony's, presently joined by the jealous gongs of St. Simon's and the Church of the Epistles. Even far off in the Hudson and the East River the sounds of the commotion were heard, and the ferry-boats and tugs and ocean liners set up sirens and whistles that sailed in melancholy cadence, now varied, now reiterated, across the whole diagonal width of the city from Riverside Drive to the gray water-fronts of the lower East Side . . .

In the centre of her landaulet sat the lady in black and lavender, chatting pleasantly first with one, then with another of that fortunate few in cutaways who had found their way to speaking distance in the first rush. After a while she glanced around her and beside her with a look of growing annoyance.

She yawned and asked the man nearest her if he couldn't run in somewhere and get her a glass of water. The man apologized in some embarrassment. He could not have moved hand or foot. He could not have scratched his own ear . . .

As the first blast of the river sirens keened along the air, Olive fastened the last safety-pin in little Arthur's rompers and looked up. Merlin saw her start, stiffen slowly like hardening stucco, and then give a little gasp of surprise and disapproval.

"That woman," she cried suddenly. "Oh!"

She flashed a glance at Merlin that mingled reproach and pain, and without another word gathered up little Arthur with one hand, grasped her husband by the other, and darted amazingly in a winding, bumping canter through the crowd. Somehow people gave way before her; somehow she managed to retain her grasp on her son and husband; somehow she managed to emerge two blocks up, battered and dishevelled, into an open space, and, without slowing up her pace, darted down a side-street. Then at last, when uproar had died away into a dim and distant clamor, did she come to a walk and set little Arthur upon his feet.

"And on Sunday, too! Hasn't she disgraced herself enough?" This was her only comment. She said it to Arthur, as she seemed to address her remarks to Arthur throughout the remainder of the day. For some curious and esoteric reason she had never once looked at her husband during the entire retreat.

IV

The years between thirty-five and sixty-five revolve before the passive mind as one unexplained, confusing merry-go-round. True, they are a merry-go-round of ill-gaited and wind-broken horses, painted first in pastel colors, then in dull grays and browns, but perplexing and intolerably dizzy the thing is, as never were the merry-go-rounds of childhood or adolescence;

as never, surely, were the certain-coursed, dynamic roller-coasters of youth. For most men and women these thirty years are taken up with a gradual withdrawal from life, a retreat first from a front with many shelters, those myriad amusements and curiosities of youth, to a line with less, when we peel down our ambitions to one ambition, our recreations to one recreation, our friends to a few to whom we are anaesthetic; ending up at last in a solitary, desolate strong point that is not strong, where the shells now whistle abominably, now are but half-heard as, by turns frightened and tired, we sit waiting for death.

At forty, then, Merlin was no different from himself at thirty-five; a larger paunch, a gray twinkling near his ears, a more certain lack of vivacity in his walk. His forty-five differed from his forty by a like margin, unless one mention a slight deafness in his left ear. But at fifty-five the process had become a chemical change of immense rapidity. Yearly he was more and more an "old man" to his family—senile almost, so far as his wife was concerned. He was by this time complete owner of the bookshop. The mysterious Mr. Moonlight Quill, dead some five years and not survived by his wife, had deeded the whole stock and store to him, and there he still spent his days, conversant now by name with almost all that man has recorded for three thousand years, a human catalogue, an authority upon tooling and binding, upon folios and first editions, an accurate inventory of a thousand authors whom he could never have understood and had certainly never read.

At sixty-five he distinctly doddered. He had assumed the melancholy habits of the aged so often portrayed by the second old man in standard Victorian comedies. He consumed vast warehouses of time searching for mislaid spectacles. He "nagged" his wife and was nagged in turn. He told the same jokes three or four times a year at the family table, and gave his son weird, impossible directions as to his conduct in life. Mentally and materially he was so entirely different from the Merlin Grainger of twenty-five that it seemed incongruous that he should bear the same name.

He worked still in the bookshop with the assistance of a youth, whom, of course, he considered very idle, indeed, and a new young woman, Miss Gaffney. Miss McCracken, ancient and unvenerable as himself, still kept the accounts. Young Arthur was gone into Wall Street to sell bonds, as all the young men seemed to be doing in that day. This, of course, was as it should be. Let old Merlin get what magic he could from his books—the place of young King Arthur was in the counting-house.

One afternoon at four when he had slipped noiselessly up to the front of the store on his soft-soled slippers, led by a newly formed habit, of which, to be fair, he was rather ashamed, of spying upon the young man clerk, he looked casually out of the front window, straining his faded eyesight to reach the street. A limousine, large, portentous, impressive, had drawn to the curb, and the chauffeur, after dismounting and holding some sort of conversation with persons in the interior of the car, turned about and advanced in a bewildered fashion toward the entrance of the Moonlight Quill. He opened the door, shuffled in, and, glancing uncertainly at the old man in the skull-cap, addressed him in a thick, murky voice, as though his words came through a fog.

"Do you—do you sell additions?"

Merlin nodded.

"The arithmetic books are in the back of the store."

The chauffeur took off his cap and scratched a close-cropped, fuzzy head.

"Oh, naw. This I want's a detecatif story." He jerked a thumb back toward the limousine. "She seen it in the paper. Firs' addition."

Merlin's interest quickened. Here was possibly a big sale.

"Oh, editions. Yes, we've advertised some firsts, but—detective stories, I—don't—believe—What was the title?"

"I forget. About a crime."

"About a crime. I have—well, I have 'The Crimes of the Borgias'—full morocco, London 1769, beautifully—"

"Naw," interrupted the chauffeur, "this was one fella did this crime. She seen you had it for sale in the paper." He rejected several possible titles with the air of connoisseur.

"'Silver Bones,'" he announced suddenly out of a slight pause.

"What?" demanded Merlin, suspecting that the stiffness of his sinews were being commented on.

"Silver Bones. That was the guy that done the crime."

"Silver Bones?"

"Silver Bones. Indian, maybe."

Merlin, stroked his grizzly cheeks. "Gees, Mister," went on the prospective purchaser, "if you wanna save me an awful bawln' out jes' try an' think. The old lady goes wile if everything don't run smooth."

But Merlin's musings on the subject of Silver Bones were as futile as his obliging search through the shelves, and five minutes later a very dejected charioteer wound his way back to his mistress. Through the glass Merlin could see the visible symbols of a tremendous uproar going on in the interior of the limousine. The chauffeur made wild, appealing gestures of his innocence, evidently to no avail, for when he turned around and climbed back into the driver's seat his expression was not a little dejected.

Then the door of the limousine opened and gave forth a pale and slender young man of about twenty, dressed in the attenuation of fashion and carrying a wisp of a cane. He entered the shop, walked past Merlin, and proceeded to take out a cigarette and light it. Merlin approached him.

"Anything I can do for you, sir?"

"Old boy," said the youth coolly, "there are seveereal things. You can first let me smoke my ciggy in here out of sight of that old lady in the limousine, who happens to be my grandmother. Her knowledge as to whether I smoke it or not before my majority happens to be a matter of five thousand dollars to me. The second thing is that you should look up your first edition of the 'Crime of Sylvester Bonnard' that you advertised in last

Sunday's *Times*. My grandmother there happens to want to take it off your hands."

Detecatif story! Crime of somebody! Silver Bones! All was explained. With a faint deprecatory chuckle, as if to say that he would have enjoyed this had life put him in the habit of enjoying anything, Merlin doddered away to the back of his shop where his treasures were kept, to get this latest investment which he had picked up rather cheaply at the sale of a big collection.

When he returned with it the young man was drawing on his cigarette and blowing out quantities of smoke with immense satisfaction.

"My God!" he said, "She keeps me so close to her the entire day running idiotic errands that this happens to be my first puff in six hours. What's the world coming to, I ask you, when a feeble old lady in the milk-toast era can dictate to a man as to his personal vices. I happen to be unwilling to be so dictated to. Let's see the book."

Merlin passed it to him tenderly and the young man, after opening it with a carelessness that gave a momentary jump to the book-dealer's heart, ran through the pages with his thumb.

"No illustrations, eh?" he commented. "Well, old boy, what's it worth? Speak up! We're willing to give you a fair price, though why I don't know."

"One hundred dollars," said Merlin with a frown.

The young man gave a startled whistle.

"Whew! Come on. You're not dealing with somebody from the cornbelt. I happen to be a city-bred man and my grandmother happens to be a city-bred woman, though I'll admit it'd take a special tax appropriation to keep her in repair. We'll give you twenty-five dollars, and let me tell you that's liberal. We've got books in our attic, up in our attic with my old play-things, that were written before the old boy that wrote this was born."

Merlin stiffened, expressing a rigid and meticulous horror.

"Did your grandmother give you twenty-five dollars to buy this with?"

"She did not. She gave me fifty, but she expects change. I know that old lady."

"You tell her," said Merlin with dignity, "that she has missed a very great bargain."

"Give you forty," urged the young man. "Come on now—be reasonable and don't try to hold us up——"

Merlin had wheeled around with the precious volume under his arm and was about to return it to its special drawer in his office when there was a sudden interruption. With unheard-of magnificence the front door burst rather than swung open, and admitted in the dark interior a regal apparition in black silk and fur which bore rapidly down upon him. The cigarette leaped from the fingers of the urban young man and he gave breath to an inadvertent "Damn!"—but it was upon Merlin that the entrance seemed to have the most remarkable and incongruous effect—so strong an effect that the greatest treasure of his shop slipped from his hand and joined the cigarette on the floor. Before him stood Caroline.

She was an old woman, an old woman remarkably preserved, unusually handsome, unusually erect, but still an old woman. Her hair was a soft, beautiful white, elaborately dressed and jewelled; her face, faintly rouged à la grande dame, showed webs of wrinkles at the edges of her eyes and two deeper lines in the form of stanchions connected her nose with the corners of her mouth. Her eyes were dim, ill natured, and querulous.

But it was Caroline without a doubt: Caroline's features though in decay; Caroline's figure, if brittle and stiff in movement; Caroline's manner, unmistakably compounded of a delightful insolence and an enviable self assurance; and, most of all, Caroline's voice, broken and shaky, yet with a ring in it that still could and did make chauffeurs want to drive laundry wagons and cause cigarettes to fall from the fingers of urban grandsons.

She stood and sniffed. Her eyes found the cigarette upon the floor.

"What's that?" she cried. The words were not a question—they were an entire litany of suspicion, accusation, confirmation, and decision. She tarried over them scarcely an instant. "Stand up!" she said to her grandson, "stand up and blow that nicotine out of your lungs!"

The young man looked at her in trepidation.

"Blow!" she commanded.

He pursed his lips feebly and blew into the air.

"Blow!" she repeated, more peremptorily than before.

He blew again, helplessly, ridiculously.

"Do you realize," she went on briskly, "that you've forfeited five thousand dollars in five minutes?"

Merlin momentarily expected the young man to fall pleading upon his knees, but such is the nobility of human nature that he remained standing—even blew again into the air, partly from nervousness, partly, no doubt, with some vague hope of reingratiating himself.

"Young ass!" cried Caroline. "Once more, just once more and you leave college and go to work."

This threat had such an overwhelming effect upon the young man that he took on an even paler pallor than was natural to him. But Caroline was not through.

"Do you think I don't know what you and your brothers, yes, and your asinine father too, think of me? Well, I do. You think I'm senile. You think I'm soft. I'm not!" She struck herself with her fist as though to prove that she was a mass of muscle and sinew. "And I'll have more brains left when you've got me laid out in the drawing-room some sunny day than you and the rest of them were born with."

"But Grandmother——"

"Be quiet. You, a thin little stick of a boy, who if it weren't for my money might have risen to be a journeyman barber out in the Bronx—Let me see your hands. Ugh! The hands of a barber—*you* presume to be smart with *me*, who once had three counts and a bona-fide duke, not to mention half a dozen papal titles pursue me from the city of Rome to the city of New York." She paused, took breath. "Stand up! Blow'!"

The young man obediently blew. Simultaneously the door opened and an excited gentleman of middle age who wore a coat and hat trimmed with fur, and seemed, moreover, to be trimmed with the same sort of fur himself on upper lip and chin, rushed into the store and up to Caroline.

"Found you at last," he cried. "Been looking for you all over town. Tried your house on the 'phone and your secretary told me he thought you'd gone to a bookshop called the Moonlight—"

Caroline turned to him irritably.

"Do I employ you for your reminiscences?" she snapped. "Are you my tutor or my broker?"

"Your broker," confessed the fur-trimmed man, taken somewhat aback. "I beg your pardon. I came about that phonograph stock. I can sell for a hundred and five."

"Then do it."

"Very well. I thought I'd better—"

"Go sell it. I'm talking to my grandson."

"Very well. I—"

"Good-by."

"Good-by, Madame." The fur-trimmed man made a slight bow and hurried in some confusion from the shop.

"As for you," said Caroline, turning to her grandson, "you stay just where you are and be quiet."

She turned to Merlin and included his entire length in a not unfriendly survey. Then she smiled and he found himself smiling too. In an instant they had both broken into a cracked but none the less spontaneous chuckle. She seized his arm and hurried him to the other side of the store. There they stopped, faced each other, and gave vent to another long fit of senile glee.

"It's the only way," she gasped in a sort of triumphant malignity. "The only thing that keeps old folks like me happy is the sense that they can make other people step around. To be old and rich and have poor descendants is almost as much fun as to be young and beautiful and have ugly sisters."

"Oh, yes," chuckled Merlin. "I know. I envy you."

She nodded, blinking.

"The last time I was in here, forty years ago," she said, "you were a young man very anxious to kick up your heels."

"I was," he confessed.

"My visit must have meant a good deal to you."

"You have all along," he exclaimed. "I thought—I used to think at first that you were a real person—human, I mean."

She laughed.

"Many men have thought me inhuman."

"But now," continued Merlin excitedly, "I understand. Understanding is allowed to us old people—after nothing much matters. I see now that on a certain night when you danced upon a table-top you were nothing but my romantic yearning for a beautiful and perverse woman."

Her old eyes were far away, her voice no more than the echo of a forgotten dream.

"How I danced that night! I remember."

"You were making an attempt at me. Olive's arms were closing about me and you warned me to be free and keep my measure of youth and irresponsibility. But it seemed like an effect gotten up at the last moment. It came too late."

"You are very old," she said inscrutably. "I did not realize."

"Also I have not forgotten what you did to me when I was thirty-five. You shook me with that traffic tie-up. It was a magnificent effort. The beauty and power you radiated! You became personified even to my wife, and she feared you. For weeks I wanted to slip out of the house at dark and forget the stuffiness of life with music and cocktails and a girl to make me young. But then—I no longer knew how."

"And now you are so very old."

With a sort of awe she moved back and away from him.

"Yes, leave me!" he cried. "You are old also; the spirit withers with the skin. Have you come here only to tell me something I had best forget: that to be old and poor is perhaps more wretched than to be old and rich; to remind me that *my* son hurls my gray failure in my face?"

"Give me my book," she commanded harshly. "Be quick, old man!"

Merlin looked at her once more and then patiently obeyed. He picked up the book and handed it to her, shaking his head when she offered him a bill.

"Why go through the farce of paying me? Once you made me wreck these very premises."

"I did," she said in anger, "and I'm glad. Perhaps there had been enough done to ruin *me*."

She gave him a glance, half disdain, half ill-concealed uneasiness, and with a brisk word to her urban grandson moved toward the door.

Then she was gone—out of his shop—out of his life. The door clicked. With a sigh he turned and walked brokenly back toward the glass partition that enclosed the yellowed accounts of many years as well as the mellowed, wrinkled Miss McCracken.

Merlin regarded her parched, cobwebbed face with an odd sort of pity. She, at any rate, had had less from life than he. No rebellious, romantic spirit popping out unbidden had, in its memorable moments, given her life a zest and a glory.

Then Miss McCracken looked up and spoke to him:

"Still a spunky old piece, isn't she?"

Merlin started.

"Who?"

"Old Alicia Dare. Mrs. Thomas Allerdyce she is now, of course; has been, these thirty years."

"What? I don't understand you." Merlin sat down suddenly in his swivel chair; his eyes were wide.

"Why, surely, Mr. Grainger, you can't tell me that you've forgotten her, when for ten years she was the most notorious character in New York. Why, one time when she was the correspondent in the Throckmorton divorce case she attracted so much attention on Fifth Avenue that there was a traffic tie-up. Didn't you read about it in the papers."

"I never used to read the papers." His ancient brain was whirring.

"Well, you can't have forgotten the time she came in here and ruined the business. Let me tell you I came near asking Mr. Moonlight Quill for my salary, and clearing out."

"Do you mean, that—that you *saw* her?"

"Saw her! How could I help it with the racket that went on. Heaven knows Mr. Moonlight Quill didn't like it either but of course *he* didn't say anything. He was daffy about her and she could twist him around her little finger. The second he opposed one of her whims she'd threaten to tell his wife on him. Served him right. The idea of that man falling for a pretty adventuress! Of course he was never rich enough for *her* even though the shop paid well in those days."

"But when I saw her," stammered Merlin, "that is, when I *thought* saw her, she lived with her mother."

"Mother, trash!" said Miss McCracken indignantly. "She had a woman there she called 'Aunty', who was no more related to her than I am. Oh, she was a bad one—but clever. Right after the Throckmorton divorce case she married Thomas Allerdyce, and made herself secure for life."

"Who was she?" cried Merlin. "For God's sake what was she—a witch?"

"Why, she was Alicia Dare, the dancer, of course. In those days you couldn't pick up a paper without finding her picture."

Merlin sat very quiet, his brain suddenly fatigued and stilled. He was an old man now indeed, so old that it was impossible for him to dream of ever having been young, so old that the glamour was gone out of the world, passing not into the faces of children and into the persistent comforts of warmth and life, but passing out of the range of sight and feeling. He was never to smile again or to sit in a long reverie when spring evenings wafted the cries of children in at his window until gradually they became the friends of his boyhood out there, urging him to come and play before the last dark came down. He was too old now even for memories.

That night he sat at supper with his wife and son, who had used him for their blind purposes. Olive said:

"Don't sit there like a death's-head. Say something."

"Let him sit quiet," growled Arthur. "If you encourage him he'll tell us a story we've heard a hundred times before."

Merlin went up-stairs very quietly at nine o'clock. When he was in his room and had closed the door tight he stood by it for a moment, his thin limbs trembling. He knew now that he had always been a fool.

"O Russet Witch!"

But it was too late. He had angered Providence by resisting too many temptations. There was nothing left but heaven, where he would meet only those who, like him, had wasted earth.

THE CURIOUS CASE
OF BENJAMIN BUTTON

First published in
Collier's, May, 1922

I

As long ago as 1860 it was the proper thing to be born at home. At present, so I am told, the high gods of medicine have decreed that the first cries of the young shall be uttered upon the anaesthetic air of a hospital, preferably a fashionable one. So young Mr. and Mrs. Roger Button were fifty years ahead of style when they decided, one day in the summer of 1860, that their first baby should be born in a hospital. Whether this anachronism had any bearing upon the astonishing history I am about to set down will never be known.

I shall tell you what occurred, and let you judge for yourself.

The Roger Buttons held an enviable position, both social and financial, in ante-bellum Baltimore. They were related to the This Family and the That Family, which, as every Southerner knew, entitled them to membership in that enormous peerage which largely populated the Confederacy. This was their first experience with the charming old custom of having babies—Mr. Button was naturally nervous. He hoped it would be a boy so that he could be sent to Yale College in Connecticut, at which institution Mr. Button himself had been known for four years by the somewhat obvious nickname of "Cuff."

On the September morning consecrated to the enormous

event he arose nervously at six o'clock, dressed himself, adjusted an impeccable stock, and hurried forth through the streets of Baltimore to the hospital, to determine whether the darkness of the night had borne in new life upon its bosom.

When he was approximately a hundred yards from the Maryland Private Hospital for Ladies and Gentlemen he saw Doctor Keene, the family physician, descending the front steps, rubbing his hands together with a washing movement—as all doctors are required to do by the unwritten ethics of their profession.

Mr. Roger Button, the president of Roger Button & Co., Wholesale Hardware, began to run toward Doctor Keene with much less dignity than was expected from a Southern gentleman of that picturesque period. "Doctor Keene!" he called. "Oh, Doctor Keene!"

The doctor heard him, faced around, and stood waiting, a curious expression settling on his harsh, medicinal face as Mr. Button drew near.

"What happened?" demanded Mr. Button, as he came up in a gasping rush. "What was it? How is she? A boy? Who is it? What—"

"Talk sense!" said Doctor Keene sharply. He appeared somewhat irritated.

"Is the child born?" begged Mr. Button.

Doctor Keene frowned. "Why, yes, I suppose so—after a fashion." Again he threw a curious glance at Mr. Button.

"Is my wife all right?"

"Yes."

"Is it a boy or a girl?"

"Here now!" cried Doctor Keene in a perfect passion of irritation, "I'll ask you to go and see for yourself. Outrageous!" He snapped the last word out in almost one syllable, then he turned away muttering: "Do you imagine a case like this will help my professional reputation? One more would ruin me—ruin anybody."

"What's the matter?" demanded Mr. Button appalled. "Triplets?"

"No, not triplets!" answered the doctor cuttingly. "What's more, you can go and see for yourself. And get another doctor. I brought you into the world, young man, and I've been physician to your family for forty years, but I'm through with you! I don't want to see you or any of your relatives ever again! Good-bye!"

Then he turned sharply, and without another word climbed into his phaeton, which was waiting at the curbstone, and drove severely away.

Mr. Button stood there upon the sidewalk, stupefied and trembling from head to foot. What horrible mishap had occurred? He had suddenly lost all desire to go into the Maryland Private Hospital for Ladies and Gentlemen—it was with the greatest difficulty that, a moment later, he forced himself to mount the steps and enter the front door.

A nurse was sitting behind a desk in the opaque gloom of the hall. Swallowing his shame, Mr. Button approached her.

"Good-morning," she remarked, looking up at him pleasantly.

"Good-morning. I—I am Mr. Button."

At this a look of utter terror spread itself over the girl's face. She rose to her feet and seemed about to fly from the hall, restraining herself only with the most apparent difficulty.

"I want to see my child," said Mr. Button.

The nurse gave a little scream. "Oh—of course!" she cried hysterically. "Upstairs. Right upstairs. Go—*up!*"

She pointed the direction, and Mr. Button, bathed in cool perspiration, turned falteringly, and began to mount to the second floor. In the upper hall he addressed another nurse who approached him, basin in hand. "I'm Mr. Button," he managed to articulate. "I want to see my——"

Clank! The basin clattered to the floor and rolled in the direction of the stairs. Clank! Clank! It began a methodical descent as if sharing in the general terror which this gentleman provoked.

"I want to see my child!" Mr. Button almost shrieked. He was on the verge of collapse.

Clank! The basin reached the first floor. The nurse regained control of herself, and threw Mr. Button a look of hearty contempt.

"All *right*, Mr. Button," she agreed in a hushed voice. "Very *well!* But if you *knew* what a state it's put us all in this morning! It's perfectly outrageous! The hospital will never have a ghost of a reputation after——"

"Hurry!" he cried hoarsely. "I can't stand this!"

"Come this way, then, Mr. Button."

He dragged himself after her. At the end of a long hall they reached a room from which proceeded a variety of howls—indeed, a room which, in later parlance, would have been known as the "crying-room." They entered.

"Well," gasped Mr. Button, "which is mine?"

"There!" said the nurse.

Mr. Button's eyes followed her pointing finger, and this is what he saw. Wrapped in a voluminous white blanket, and partly crammed into one of the cribs, there sat an old man apparently about seventy years of age. His sparse hair was almost white, and from his chin dripped a long smoke-coloured beard, which waved absurdly back and forth, fanned by the breeze coming in at the window. He looked up at Mr. Button with dim, faded eyes in which lurked a puzzled question.

"Am I mad?" thundered Mr. Button, his terror resolving into rage. "Is this some ghastly hospital joke?

"It doesn't seem like a joke to us," replied the nurse severely. "And I don't know whether you're mad or not—but that is most certainly your child."

The cool perspiration redoubled on Mr. Button's forehead. He closed his eyes, and then, opening them, looked again. There was no mistake—he was gazing at a man of threescore and ten—a *baby* of threescore and ten, a baby whose feet hung over the sides of the crib in which it was reposing.

The old man looked placidly from one to the other for a moment, and then suddenly spoke in a cracked and ancient voice. "Are you my father?" he demanded.

Mr. Button and the nurse started violently.

"Because if you are," went on the old man querulously, "I wish you'd get me out of this place—or, at least, get them to put a comfortable rocker in here."

"Where in God's name did you come from? Who are you?" burst out Mr. Button frantically.

"I can't tell you *exactly* who I am," replied the querulous whine, "because I've only been born a few hours—but my last name is certainly Button."

"You lie! You're an impostor!"

The old man turned wearily to the nurse. "Nice way to welcome a new-born child," he complained in a weak voice. "Tell him he's wrong, why don't you?"

"You're wrong, Mr. Button," said the nurse severely. "This is your child, and you'll have to make the best of it. We're going to ask you to take him home with you as soon as possible—some time to-day."

"Home?" repeated Mr. Button incredulously.

"Yes, we can't have him here. We really can't, you know?"

"I'm right glad of it," whined the old man. "This is a fine place to keep a youngster of quiet tastes. With all this yelling and howling, I haven't been able to get a wink of sleep. I asked for something to eat"—here his voice rose to a shrill note of protest—"and they brought me a bottle of milk!"

Mr. Button, sank down upon a chair near his son and concealed his face in his hands. "My heavens!" he murmured, in an ecstasy of horror. "What will people say? What must I do?"

"You'll have to take him home," insisted the nurse— "immediately!"

A grotesque picture formed itself with dreadful clarity before the eyes of the tortured man—a picture of himself walking through the crowded streets of the city with this appalling apparition stalking by his side.

"I can't. I can't," he moaned.

People would stop to speak to him, and what was he going to say? He would have to introduce this—this septuagenarian: "This is my son, born early this morning." And then the old man would gather his blanket around him and they would plod on, past the bustling stores, the slave market—for a dark instant Mr. Button wished passionately that his son was black—past the luxurious houses of the residential district, past the home for the aged . . .

"Come! Pull yourself together," commanded the nurse.

"See here," the old man announced suddenly, "if you think I'm going to walk home in this blanket, you're entirely mistaken."

"Babies always have blankets."

With a malicious crackle the old man held up a small white swaddling garment. "Look!" he quavered. "*This* is what they had ready for me."

"Babies always wear those," said the nurse primly.

"Well," said the old man, "this baby's not going to wear anything in about two minutes. This blanket itches. They might at least have given me a sheet."

"Keep it on! Keep it on!" said Mr. Button hurriedly. He turned to the nurse. "What'll I do?"

"Go down town and buy your son some clothes."

Mr. Button's son's voice followed him down into the hall: "And a cane, father. I want to have a cane."

Mr. Button banged the outer door savagely . . .

II

"Good-morning," Mr. Button said nervously, to the clerk in the Chesapeake Dry Goods Company. "I want to buy some clothes for my child."

"How old is your child, sir?"

"About six hours," answered Mr. Button, without due consideration.

"Babies' supply department in the rear."

"Why, I don't think—I'm not sure that's what I want. It's—he's an unusually large-size child. Exceptionally—ah large."

"They have the largest child's sizes."

"Where is the boys' department?" inquired Mr. Button, shifting his ground desperately. He felt that the clerk must surely scent his shameful secret.

"Right here."

"Well——" He hesitated. The notion of dressing his son in men's clothes was repugnant to him. If, say, he could only find a very large boy's suit, he might cut off that long and awful beard, dye the white hair brown, and thus manage to conceal the worst, and to retain something of his own self-respect—not to mention his position in Baltimore society.

But a frantic inspection of the boys' department revealed no suits to fit the new-born Button. He blamed the store, of course—in such cases it is the thing to blame the store.

"How old did you say that boy of yours was?" demanded the clerk curiously.

"He's—sixteen."

"Oh, I beg your pardon. I thought you said six *hours*. You'll find the youths' department in the next aisle."

Mr. Button turned miserably away. Then he stopped, brightened, and pointed his finger toward a dressed dummy in the window display. "There!" he exclaimed. "I'll take that suit, out there on the dummy."

The clerk stared. "Why," he protested, "that's not a child's suit.

At least it *is*, but it's for fancy dress. You could wear it yourself!"

"Wrap it up," insisted his customer nervously. "That's what I want."

The astonished clerk obeyed.

Back at the hospital Mr. Button entered the nursery and almost threw the package at his son. "Here's your clothes," he snapped out.

The old man untied the package and viewed the contents with a quizzical eye.

"They look sort of funny to me," he complained, "I don't want to be made a monkey of—"

"You've made a monkey of me!" retorted Mr. Button fiercely. "Never you mind how funny you look. Put them on—or I'll—or I'll *spank* you." He swallowed uneasily at the penultimate word, feeling nevertheless that it was the proper thing to say.

"All right, father"—this with a grotesque simulation of filial respect—"you've lived longer; you know best. Just as you say."

As before, the sound of the word "father" caused Mr. Button to start violently.

"And hurry."

"I'm hurrying, father."

When his son was dressed Mr. Button regarded him with depression. The costume consisted of dotted socks, pink pants, and a belted blouse with a wide white collar. Over the latter waved the long whitish beard, drooping almost to the waist. The effect was not good.

"Wait!"

Mr. Button seized a hospital shears and with three quick snaps amputated a large section of the beard. But even with this improvement the ensemble fell far short of perfection. The remaining brush of scraggly hair, the watery eyes, the ancient teeth, seemed oddly out of tone with the gaiety of the costume. Mr. Button, however, was obdurate—he held out his hand. "Come along!" he said sternly.

His son took the hand trustingly. "What are you going to call me, dad?" he quavered as they walked from the nursery—"just 'baby' for a while? till you think of a better name?"

Mr. Button grunted. "I don't know," he answered harshly. "I think we'll call you Methuselah."

III

Even after the new addition to the Button family had had his hair cut short and then dyed to a sparse unnatural black, had had his face shaved so close that it glistened, and had been attired in small-boy clothes made to order by a flabbergasted tailor, it was impossible for Button to ignore the fact that his son was a poor excuse for a first family baby. Despite his aged stoop, Benjamin Button—for it was by this name they called him instead of by the appropriate but invidious Methuselah—was five feet eight inches tall. His clothes did not conceal this, nor did the clipping and dyeing of his eyebrows disguise the fact that the eyes underneath were faded and watery and tired. In fact, the baby-nurse who had been engaged in advance left the house after one look, in a state of considerable indignation.

But Mr. Button persisted in his unwavering purpose. Benjamin was a baby, and a baby he should remain. At first he declared that if Benjamin didn't like warm milk he could go without food altogether, but he was finally prevailed upon to allow his son bread and butter, and even oatmeal by way of a compromise. One day he brought home a rattle and, giving it to Benjamin, insisted in no uncertain terms that he should "play with it," whereupon the old man took it with a weary expression and could be heard jingling it obediently at intervals throughout the day.

There can be no doubt, though, that the rattle bored him, and that he found other and more soothing amusements when he was left alone. For instance, Mr. Button discovered one day that during the preceding week he had smoked more cigars than ever before—a phenomenon, which was explained a few days later when, entering the nursery unexpectedly, he found the room full of faint blue haze and Benjamin, with a guilty expression on his face, trying to conceal the butt of a dark Havana. This, of course, called for a severe spanking, but Mr. Button found that he could not bring himself to administer it. He merely warned his son that he would "stunt his growth."

Nevertheless he persisted in his attitude. He brought home lead soldiers, he brought toy trains, he brought large pleasant animals made of cotton, and, to perfect the illusion which he was creating—for himself at least—he passionately demanded of the clerk in the toy-store whether "the paint would come oft the pink duck if the baby put it in his mouth." But, despite all his father's efforts, Benjamin refused to be interested. He would steal down the back stairs and return to the nursery with a volume of the Encyclopedia Britannica, over which he would pore through an afternoon, while his cotton cows and his Noah's ark were left neglected on the floor. Against such a stubbornness Mr. Button's efforts were of little avail.

The sensation created in Baltimore was, at first, prodigious. What the mishap would have cost the Buttons and their kinsfolk socially cannot be determined, for the outbreak of the Civil War drew the city's attention to other things. A few people who were unfailingly polite racked their brains for compliments to give to the parents—and finally hit upon the ingenious device of declaring that the baby resembled his grandfather, a fact which, due to the standard state of decay common to all men of seventy, could not be denied. Mr. and Mrs. Roger Button were not pleased, and Benjamin's grandfather was furiously insulted.

Benjamin, once he left the hospital, took life as he found it. Several small boys were brought to see him, and he spent a stiff-jointed afternoon trying to work up an interest in tops and marbles—he even managed, quite accidentally, to break a kitchen window with a stone from a sling shot, a feat which secretly delighted his father.

Thereafter Benjamin contrived to break something every day, but he did these things only because they were expected of him, and because he was by nature obliging.

When his grandfather's initial antagonism wore off, Benjamin and that gentleman took enormous pleasure in one another's company. They would sit for hours, these two, so far apart in age and experience, and, like old cronies, discuss with tireless monotony the slow events of the day. Benjamin felt more at ease in his grandfather's presence than in his parents'—they seemed always somewhat in awe of him and, despite the dictatorial authority they exercised over him, frequently addressed him as "Mr."

He was as puzzled as any one else at the apparently advanced age of his mind and body at birth. He read up on it in the medical journal, but found that no such case had been previously recorded. At his father's urging he made an honest attempt to play with other boys, and frequently he joined in the milder games—football shook him up too much, and he feared that in case of a fracture his ancient bones would refuse to knit.

When he was five he was sent to kindergarten, where he was initiated into the art of pasting green paper on orange paper, of weaving coloured maps and manufacturing eternal cardboard necklaces. He was inclined to drowse off to sleep in the middle of these tasks, a habit which both irritated and frightened his young teacher.

To his relief she complained to his parents, and he was removed from the school. The Roger Buttons told their friends that they felt he was too young.

By the time he was twelve years old his parents had grown used to him. Indeed, so strong is the force of custom that they no longer felt that he was different from any other child—except when some curious anomaly reminded them of the fact. But one day a few weeks after his twelfth birthday, while looking in the mirror, Benjamin made, or thought he made, an astonishing discovery. Did his eyes deceive him, or had his hair turned in the dozen years of his life from white to iron-gray under its concealing dye? Was the network of wrinkles on his face becoming less pronounced? Was his skin healthier and firmer, with even a touch of ruddy winter colour? He could not tell. He knew that he no longer stooped, and that his physical condition had improved since the early days of his life.

"Can it be——?" he thought to himself, or, rather, scarcely dared to think.

He went to his father. "I am grown," he announced determinedly. "I want to put on long trousers."

His father hesitated. "Well," he said finally, "I don't know. Fourteen is the age for putting on long trousers—and you are only twelve."

"But you'll have to admit," protested Benjamin, "that I'm big for my age."

His father looked at him with illusory speculation. "Oh, I'm not so sure of that," he said. "I was as big as you when I was twelve."

This was not true—it was all part of Roger Button's silent agreement with himself to believe in his son's normality.

Finally a compromise was reached. Benjamin was to continue to dye his hair. He was to make a better attempt to play with boys of his own age. He was not to wear his spectacles or carry a cane in the street. In return for these concessions he was allowed his first suit of long trousers . . .

IV

Of the life of Benjamin Button between his twelfth and twenty-first year I intend to say little. Suffice to record that they were years of normal ungrowth. When Benjamin was eighteen he was erect as a man of fifty; he had more hair and it was of a dark gray; his step was firm, his voice had lost its cracked quaver and descended to a healthy baritone. So his father sent him up to

Connecticut to take examinations for entrance to Yale College. Benjamin passed his examination and became a member of the freshman class.

On the third day following his matriculation he received a notification from Mr. Hart, the college registrar, to call at his office and arrange his schedule. Benjamin, glancing in the mirror, decided that his hair needed a new application of its brown dye, but an anxious inspection of his bureau drawer disclosed that the dye bottle was not there. Then he remembered—he had emptied it the day before and thrown it away.

He was in a dilemma. He was due at the registrar's in five minutes. There seemed to be no help for it—he must go as he was. He did.

"Good-morning," said the registrar politely. "You've come to inquire about your son."

"Why, as a matter of fact, my name's Button——" began Benjamin, but Mr. Hart cut him off.

"I'm very glad to meet you, Mr. Button. I'm expecting your son here any minute."

"That's me!" burst out Benjamin. "I'm a freshman."

"What!"

"I'm a freshman."

"Surely you're joking."

"Not at all."

The registrar frowned and glanced at a card before him. "Why, I have Mr. Benjamin Button's age down here as eighteen."

"That's my age," asserted Benjamin, flushing slightly.

The registrar eyed him wearily. "Now surely, Mr. Button, you don't expect me to believe that."

Benjamin smiled wearily. "I am eighteen," he repeated.

The registrar pointed sternly to the door. "Get out," he said. "Get out of college and get out of town. You are a dangerous lunatic."

"I am eighteen."

Mr. Hart opened the door. "The idea!" he shouted. "A man of

your age trying to enter here as a freshman. Eighteen years old, are you? Well, I'll give you eighteen minutes to get out of town."

Benjamin Button walked with dignity from the room, and half a dozen undergraduates, who were waiting in the hall, followed him curiously with their eyes. When he had gone a little way he turned around, faced the infuriated registrar, who was still standing in the door-way, and repeated in a firm voice: "I am eighteen years old."

To a chorus of titters which went up from the group of undergraduates, Benjamin walked away.

But he was not fated to escape so easily. On his melancholy walk to the railroad station he found that he was being followed by a group, then by a swarm, and finally by a dense mass of undergraduates. The word had gone around that a lunatic had passed the entrance examinations for Yale and attempted to palm himself off as a youth of eighteen. A fever of excitement permeated the college. Men ran hatless out of classes, the football team abandoned its practice and joined the mob, professors' wives with bonnets awry and bustles out of position, ran shouting after the procession, from which proceeded a continual succession of remarks aimed at the tender sensibilities of Benjamin Button.

"He must be the wandering Jew!"

"He ought to go to prep school at his age!"

"Look at the infant prodigy!"

"He thought this was the old men's home."

"Go up to Harvard!"

Benjamin increased his gait, and soon he was running. He would show them! He *would* go to Harvard, and then they would regret these ill-considered taunts!

Safely on board the train for Baltimore, he put his head from the window. "You'll regret this!" he shouted.

"Ha-ha!" the undergraduates laughed. "Ha-ha-ha!" It was the biggest mistake that Yale College had ever made . . .

V

In 1880 Benjamin Button was twenty years old, and he signalised his birthday by going to work for his father in Roger Button & Co., Wholesale Hardware. It was in that same year that he began "going out socially"—that is, his father insisted on taking him to several fashionable dances. Roger Button was now fifty, and he and his son were more and more companionable—in fact, since Benjamin had ceased to dye his hair (which was still grayish) they appeared about the same age, and could have passed for brothers.

One night in August they got into the phaeton attired in their full-dress suits and drove out to a dance at the Shevlins' country house, situated just outside of Baltimore. It was a gorgeous evening. A full moon drenched the road to the lustreless colour of platinum, and late-blooming harvest flowers breathed into the motionless air aromas that were like low, half-heard laughter. The open country, carpeted for rods around with bright wheat, was translucent as in the day. It was almost impossible not to be affected by the sheer beauty of the sky—almost.

"There's a great future in the dry-goods business," Roger Button was saying. He was not a spiritual man—his aesthetic sense was rudimentary.

"Old fellows like me can't learn new tricks," he observed profoundly. "It's you youngsters with energy and vitality that have the great future before you."

Far up the road the lights of the Shevlins' country house drifted into view, and presently there was a sighing sound that crept persistently toward them—it might have been the fine plaint of violins or the rustle of the silver wheat under the moon.

They pulled up behind a handsome brougham whose passengers were disembarking at the door. A lady got out, then an elderly gentleman, then another young lady, beautiful as sin. Benjamin started; an almost chemical change seemed to dissolve and recompose the very elements of his body. A rigour passed over him, blood rose into his cheeks, his forehead, and there was a steady thumping in his ears. It was first love.

The girl was slender and frail, with hair that was ashen under the moon and honey-coloured under the sputtering gas-lamps of the porch. Over her shoulders was thrown a Spanish mantilla of softest yellow, butterflied in black; her feet were glittering buttons at the hem of her bustled dress.

Roger Button leaned over to his son. "That," he said, "is young Hildegarde Moncrief, the daughter of General Moncrief."

Benjamin nodded coldly. "Pretty little thing," he said indifferently. But when the negro boy had led the buggy away, he added: "Dad, you might introduce me to her."

They approached a group, of which Miss Moncrief was the centre. Reared in the old tradition, she curtsied low before Benjamin. Yes, he might have a dance. He thanked her and walked away—staggered away.

The interval until the time for his turn should arrive dragged itself out interminably. He stood close to the wall, silent, inscrutable, watching with murderous eyes the young bloods of Baltimore as they eddied around Hildegarde Moncrief, passionate admiration in their faces. How obnoxious they seemed to Benjamin; how intolerably rosy! Their curling brown whiskers aroused in him a feeling equivalent to indigestion.

But when his own time came, and he drifted with her out upon the changing floor to the music of the latest waltz from Paris, his jealousies and anxieties melted from him like a mantle of snow. Blind with enchantment, he felt that life was just beginning.

"You and your brother got here just as we did, didn't you?" asked Hildegarde, looking up at him with eyes that were like bright blue enamel.

Benjamin hesitated. If she took him for his father's brother, would it be best to enlighten her? He remembered his experience at Yale, so he decided against it. It would be rude to contradict a lady; it would be criminal to mar this exquisite occasion with the grotesque story of his origin. Later, perhaps. So he nodded, smiled, listened, was happy.

"I like men of your age," Hildegarde told him. "Young boys are so idiotic. They tell me how much champagne they drink at college, and how much money they lose playing cards. Men of your age know how to appreciate women."

Benjamin felt himself on the verge of a proposal—with an effort he choked back the impulse. "You're just the romantic age," she continued—"fifty. Twenty-five is too worldly-wise; thirty is apt to be pale from overwork; forty is the age of long stories that take a whole cigar to tell; sixty is—oh, sixty is too near seventy; but fifty is the mellow age. I love fifty."

Fifty seemed to Benjamin a glorious age. He longed passionately to be fifty.

"I've always said," went on Hildegarde, "that I'd rather marry a man of fifty and be taken care of than marry a man of thirty and take care of *him*."

For Benjamin the rest of the evening was bathed in a honey-coloured mist. Hildegarde gave him two more dances, and they discovered that they were marvellously in accord on all the questions of the day. She was to go driving with him on the following Sunday, and then they would discuss all these questions further.

Going home in the phaeton just before the crack of dawn, when the first bees were humming and the fading moon glimmered in the cool dew, Benjamin knew vaguely that his father was discussing wholesale hardware.

" . . . And what do you think should merit our biggest attention after hammers and nails?" the elder Button was saying.

"Love," replied Benjamin absent-mindedly.

"Lugs?" exclaimed Roger Button, "Why, I've just covered the question of lugs."

Benjamin regarded him with dazed eyes just as the eastern sky was suddenly cracked with light, and an oriole yawned piercingly in the quickening trees . . .

VI

When, six months later, the engagement of Miss Hildegarde Moncrief to Mr. Benjamin Button was made known (I say "made known," for General Moncrief declared he would rather fall upon his sword than announce it), the excitement in Baltimore society reached a feverish pitch. The almost forgotten story of Benjamin's birth was remembered and sent out upon the winds of scandal in picaresque and incredible forms. It was said that Benjamin was really the father of Roger Button, that he was his brother who had been in prison for forty years, that he was John Wilkes Booth in disguise—and, finally, that he had two small conical horns sprouting from his head.

The Sunday supplements of the New York papers played up the case with fascinating sketches which showed the head of Benjamin Button attached to a fish, to a snake, and, finally, to a body of solid brass. He became known, journalistically, as the Mystery Man of Maryland. But the true story, as is usually the case, had a very small circulation.

However, every one agreed with General Moncrief that it was "criminal" for a lovely girl who could have married any beau in Baltimore to throw herself into the arms of a man who was assuredly fifty. In vain Mr. Roger Button published his son's birth certificate in large type in the Baltimore *Blaze*. No one believed it. You had only to look at Benjamin and see.

On the part of the two people most concerned there was no wavering. So many of the stories about her fiancé were false that Hildegarde refused stubbornly to believe even the true one. In vain General Moncrief pointed out to her the high mortality among men of fifty—or, at least, among men who looked fifty; in vain he told her of the instability of the wholesale hardware business. Hildegarde had chosen to marry for mellowness, and marry she did . . .

VII

In one particular, at least, the friends of Hildegarde Moncrief were mistaken. The wholesale hardware business prospered amazingly. In the fifteen years between Benjamin Button's marriage in 1880 and his father's retirement in 1895, the family fortune was doubled—and this was due largely to the younger member of the firm.

Needless to say, Baltimore eventually received the couple to its bosom. Even old General Moncrief became reconciled to his son-in-law when Benjamin gave him the money to bring out his *History of the Civil War* in twenty volumes, which had been refused by nine prominent publishers.

In Benjamin himself fifteen years had wrought many changes. It seemed to him that the blood flowed with new vigour through his veins. It began to be a pleasure to rise in the morning, to walk with an active step along the busy, sunny street, to work untiringly with his shipments of hammers and his cargoes of nails. It was in 1890 that he executed his famous business coup: he brought up the suggestion that *all nails used in nailing up the boxes in which nails are shipped are the property of the shippee*, a proposal which became a statute, was approved by Chief Justice Fossile, and saved Roger Button and Company, Wholesale Hardware, more than *six hundred nails every year*.

In addition, Benjamin discovered that he was becoming more and more attracted by the gay side of life. It was typical of his growing enthusiasm for pleasure that he was the first man in the city of Baltimore to own and run an automobile. Meeting him on the street, his contemporaries would stare enviously at the picture he made of health and vitality.

"He seems to grow younger every year," they would remark. And if old Roger Button, now sixty-five years old, had failed at first to give a proper welcome to his son he atoned at last by bestowing on him what amounted to adulation.

And here we come to an unpleasant subject which it will

be well to pass over as quickly as possible. There was only one thing that worried Benjamin Button; his wife had ceased to attract him.

At that time Hildegarde was a woman of thirty-five, with a son, Roscoe, fourteen years old. In the early days of their marriage Benjamin had worshipped her. But, as the years passed, her honey-coloured hair became an unexciting brown, the blue enamel of her eyes assumed the aspect of cheap crockery—moreover, and, most of all, she had become too settled in her ways, too placid, too content, too anaemic in her excitements, and too sober in her taste. As a bride it had been she who had "dragged" Benjamin to dances and dinners—now conditions were reversed. She went out socially with him, but without enthusiasm, devoured already by that eternal inertia which comes to live with each of us one day and stays with us to the end.

Benjamin's discontent waxed stronger. At the outbreak of the Spanish-American War in 1898 his home had for him so little charm that he decided to join the army. With his business influence he obtained a commission as captain, and proved so adaptable to the work that he was made a major, and finally a lieutenant-colonel just in time to participate in the celebrated charge up San Juan Hill. He was slightly wounded, and received a medal.

Benjamin had become so attached to the activity and excitement of array life that he regretted to give it up, but his business required attention, so he resigned his commission and came home. He was met at the station by a brass band and escorted to his house.

VIII

Hildegarde, waving a large silk flag, greeted him on the porch, and even as he kissed her he felt with a sinking of the heart that these three years had taken their toll. She was a woman of forty now, with a faint skirmish line of gray hairs in her head. The sight depressed him.

Up in his room he saw his reflection in the familiar mirror—he went closer and examined his own face with anxiety, comparing it after a moment with a photograph of himself in uniform taken just before the war.

"Good Lord!" he said aloud. The process was continuing. There was no doubt of it—he looked now like a man of thirty. Instead of being delighted, he was uneasy—he was growing younger. He had hitherto hoped that once he reached a bodily age equivalent to his age in years, the grotesque phenomenon which had marked his birth would cease to function. He shuddered. His destiny seemed to him awful, incredible.

When he came downstairs Hildegarde was waiting for him. She appeared annoyed, and he wondered if she had at last discovered that there was something amiss. It was with an effort to relieve the tension between them that he broached the matter at dinner in what he considered a delicate way.

"Well," he remarked lightly, "everybody says I look younger than ever."

Hildegarde regarded him with scorn. She sniffed. "Do you think it's anything to boast about?"

"I'm not boasting," he asserted uncomfortably. She sniffed again. "The idea," she said, and after a moment: "I should think you'd have enough pride to stop it."

"How can I?" he demanded.

"I'm not going to argue with you," she retorted. "But there's a right way of doing things and a wrong way. If you've made up your mind to be different from everybody else, I don't suppose I can stop you, but I really don't think it's very considerate."

"But, Hildegarde, I can't help it."

"You can too. You're simply stubborn. You think you don't want to be like any one else. You always have been that way, and you always will be. But just think how it would be if every one else looked at things as you do—what would the world be like?"

As this was an inane and unanswerable argument Benjamin made no reply, and from that time on a chasm began to widen between them. He wondered what possible fascination she had ever exercised over him.

To add to the breach, he found, as the new century gathered headway, that his thirst for gaiety grew stronger. Never a party of any kind in the city of Baltimore but he was there, dancing with the prettiest of the young married women, chatting with the most popular of the débutantes, and finding their company charming, while his wife, a dowager of evil omen, sat among the chaperons, now in haughty disapproval, and now following him with solemn, puzzled, and reproachful eyes.

"Look!" people would remark. "What a pity! A young fellow that age tied to a woman of forty-five. He must be twenty years younger than his wife." They had forgotten—as people inevitably forget—that back in 1880 their mammas and papas had also remarked about this same ill-matched pair.

Benjamin's growing unhappiness at home was compensated for by his many new interests. He took up golf and made a great success of it. He went in for dancing: in 1906 he was an expert at "The Boston," and in 1908 he was considered proficient at the "Maxine," while in 1909 his "Castle Walk" was the envy of every young man in town.

His social activities, of course, interfered to some extent with his business, but then he had worked hard at wholesale hardware for twenty-five years and felt that he could soon hand it on to his son, Roscoe, who had recently graduated from Harvard.

He and his son were, in fact, often mistaken for each other. This pleased Benjamin—he soon forgot the insidious fear which had come over him on his return from the Spanish-American

War, and grew to take a naïve pleasure in his appearance. There was only one fly in the delicious ointment—he hated to appear in public with his wife. Hildegarde was almost fifty, and the sight of her made him feel absurd . . .

IX

One September day in 1910—a few years after Roger Button & Co., Wholesale Hardware, had been handed over to young Roscoe Button—a man, apparently about twenty years old, entered himself as a freshman at Harvard University in Cambridge. He did not make the mistake of announcing that he would never see fifty again, nor did he mention the fact that his son had been graduated from the same institution ten years before.

He was admitted, and almost immediately attained a prominent position in the class, partly because he seemed a little older than the other freshmen, whose average age was about eighteen.

But his success was largely due to the fact that in the football game with Yale he played so brilliantly, with so much dash and with such a cold, remorseless anger that he scored seven touchdowns and fourteen field goals for Harvard, and caused one entire eleven of Yale men to be carried singly from the field, unconscious. He was the most celebrated man in college.

Strange to say, in his third or junior year he was scarcely able to "make" the team. The coaches said that he had lost weight, and it seemed to the more observant among them that he was not quite as tall as before. He made no touchdowns— indeed, he was retained on the team chiefly in hope that his enormous reputation would bring terror and disorganisation to the Yale team.

In his senior year he did not make the team at all. He had grown so slight and frail that one day he was taken by some sophomores for a freshman, an incident which humiliated him terribly. He became known as something of a prodigy—a senior who was surely no more than sixteen—and he was often shocked at the worldliness of some of his classmates. His studies seemed harder to him—he felt that they were too advanced. He had heard his classmates speak of St. Midas's, the famous preparatory school, at which so many of them had prepared for college, and he determined after his graduation to enter himself at St. Midas's, where the sheltered life among boys his own size would be more congenial to him.

Upon his graduation in 1914 he went home to Baltimore with his Harvard diploma in his pocket. Hildegarde was now residing in Italy, so Benjamin went to live with his son, Roscoe. But though he was welcomed in a general way there was obviously no heartiness in Roscoe's feeling toward him—there was even perceptible a tendency on his son's part to think that Benjamin, as he moped about the house in adolescent mooniness, was somewhat in the way. Roscoe was married now and prominent in Baltimore life, and he wanted no scandal to creep out in connection with his family.

Benjamin, no longer *persona grata* with the débutantes and younger college set, found himself left much alone, except for the companionship of three or four fifteen-year-old boys in the neighbourhood. His idea of going to St. Midas's school recurred to him.

"Say," he said to Roscoe one day, "I've told you over and over that I want to go to prep school."

"Well, go, then," replied Roscoe shortly. The matter was distasteful to him, and he wished to avoid a discussion.

"I can't go alone," said Benjamin helplessly. "You'll have to enter me and take me up there."

"I haven't got time," declared Roscoe abruptly. His eyes narrowed and he looked uneasily at his father. "As a matter of fact," he added, "you'd better not go on with this business much longer. You better pull up short. You better—you better"—he paused and his face crimsoned as he sought for words—"you better turn right around and start back the other way. This has gone too far to be a joke. It isn't funny any longer. You—you behave yourself!"

Benjamin looked at him, on the verge of tears.

"And another thing," continued Roscoe, "when visitors are in the house I want you to call me 'Uncle'—not 'Roscoe,' but 'Uncle,' do you understand? It looks absurd for a boy of fifteen to call me by my first name. Perhaps you'd better call me 'Uncle' *all* the time, so you'll get used to it."

With a harsh look at his father, Roscoe turned away . . .

X

At the termination of this interview, Benjamin wandered dismally upstairs and stared at himself in the mirror. He had not shaved for three months, but he could find nothing on his face but a faint white down with which it seemed unnecessary to meddle. When he had first come home from Harvard, Roscoe had approached him with the proposition that he should wear eye-glasses and imitation whiskers glued to his cheeks, and it had seemed for a moment that the farce of his early years was to be repeated. But whiskers had itched and made him ashamed. He wept and Roscoe had reluctantly relented.

Benjamin opened a book of boys' stories, *The Boy Scouts in Bimini Bay*, and began to read. But he found himself thinking persistently about the war. America had joined the Allied cause during the preceding month, and Benjamin wanted to enlist, but, alas, sixteen was the minimum age, and he did not look that old. His true age, which was fifty-seven, would have disqualified him, anyway.

There was a knock at his door, and the butler appeared with a letter bearing a large official legend in the corner and addressed to Mr. Benjamin Button. Benjamin tore it open eagerly, and read the enclosure with delight. It informed him that many reserve officers who had served in the Spanish-American War were being called back into service with a higher rank, and it enclosed his commission as brigadier-general in the United States army with orders to report immediately.

Benjamin jumped to his feet fairly quivering with enthusiasm. This was what he had wanted. He seized his cap, and ten minutes later he had entered a large tailoring establishment on Charles Street, and asked in his uncertain treble to be measured for a uniform.

"Want to play soldier, sonny?" demanded a clerk casually.

Benjamin flushed. "Say! Never mind what I want!" he retorted angrily. "My name's Button and I live on Mt. Vernon Place, so you know I'm good for it."

"Well," admitted the clerk hesitantly, "if you're not, I guess your daddy is, all right."

Benjamin was measured, and a week later his uniform was completed. He had difficulty in obtaining the proper general's insignia because the dealer kept insisting to Benjamin that a nice V.W.C.A. badge would look just as well and be much more fun to play with.

Saying nothing to Roscoe, he left the house one night and proceeded by train to Camp Mosby, in South Carolina, where he was to command an infantry brigade. On a sultry April day he approached the entrance to the camp, paid off the taxicab which had brought him from the station, and turned to the sentry on guard.

"Get some one to handle my luggage!" he said briskly.

The sentry eyed him reproachfully. "Say," he remarked, "where you goin' with the general's duds, sonny?"

Benjamin, veteran of the Spanish-American War, whirled upon him with fire in his eye, but with, alas, a changing treble voice.

"Come to attention!" he tried to thunder; he paused for breath—then suddenly he saw the sentry snap his heels together and bring his rifle to the present. Benjamin concealed a smile of gratification, but when he glanced around his smile faded. It was not he who had inspired obedience, but an imposing artillery colonel who was approaching on horseback.

"Colonel!" called Benjamin shrilly.

The colonel came up, drew rein, and looked coolly down at him with a twinkle in his eyes. "Whose little boy are you?" he demanded kindly.

"I'll soon darn well show you whose little boy I am!" retorted Benjamin in a ferocious voice. "Get down off that horse!"

The colonel roared with laughter.

"You want him, eh, general?"

"Here!" cried Benjamin desperately. "Read this." And he thrust his commission toward the colonel.

The colonel read it, his eyes popping from their sockets.

"Where'd you get this?" he demanded, slipping the document into his own pocket.

"I got it from the Government, as you'll soon find out!"

"You come along with me," said the colonel with a peculiar look. "We'll go up to headquarters and talk this over. Come along."

The colonel turned and began walking his horse in the direction of headquarters. There was nothing for Benjamin to do but follow with as much dignity as possible—meanwhile promising himself a stern revenge.

But this revenge did not materialise. Two days later, however, his son Roscoe materialised from Baltimore, hot and cross from a hasty trip, and escorted the weeping general, *sans* uniform, back to his home.

XI

In 1920 Roscoe Button's first child was born. During the attendant festivities, however, no one thought it "the thing" to mention, that the little grubby boy, apparently about ten years of age who played around the house with lead soldiers and a miniature circus, was the new baby's own grandfather.

No one disliked the little boy whose fresh, cheerful face was crossed with just a hint of sadness, but to Roscoe Button his presence was a source of torment. In the idiom of his generation Roscoe did not consider the matter "efficient." It seemed to him that his father, in refusing to look sixty, had not behaved like a "red-blooded he-man"—this was Roscoe's favourite expression—but in a curious and perverse manner. Indeed, to think about the matter for as much as a half an hour drove him to the edge of insanity. Roscoe believed that "live wires" should keep young, but carrying it out on such a scale was—was—was inefficient. And there Roscoe rested.

Five years later Roscoe's little boy had grown old enough to play childish games with little Benjamin under the supervision of the same nurse. Roscoe took them both to kindergarten on the same day, and Benjamin found that playing with little strips of coloured paper, making mats and chains and curious and beautiful designs, was the most fascinating game in the world. Once he was bad and had to stand in the corner—then he cried—but for the most part there were gay hours in the cheerful room, with the sunlight coming in the windows and Miss Bailey's kind hand resting for a moment now and then in his tousled hair.

Roscoe's son moved up into the first grade after a year, but Benjamin stayed on in the kindergarten. He was very happy. Sometimes when other tots talked about what they would do when they grew up a shadow would cross his little face as if in a dim, childish way he realised that those were things in which he was never to share.

The days flowed on in monotonous content. He went back

a third year to the kindergarten, but he was too little now to understand what the bright shining strips of paper were for. He cried because the other boys were bigger than he, and he was afraid of them. The teacher talked to him, but though he tried to understand he could not understand at all.

He was taken from the kindergarten. His nurse, Nana, in her starched gingham dress, became the centre of his tiny world. On bright days they walked in the park; Nana would point at a great gray monster and say "elephant," and Benjamin would say it after her, and when he was being undressed for bed that night he would say it over and over aloud to her: "Elyphant, elyphant, elyphant." Sometimes Nana let him jump on the bed, which was fun, because if you sat down exactly right it would bounce you up on your feet again, and if you said "Ah" for a long time while you jumped you got a very pleasing broken vocal effect.

He loved to take a big cane from the hat-rack and go around hitting chairs and tables with it and saying: "Fight, fight, fight." When there were people there the old ladies would cluck at him, which interested him, and the young ladies would try to kiss him, which he submitted to with mild boredom. And when the long day was done at five o'clock he would go upstairs with Nana and be fed on oatmeal and nice soft mushy foods with a spoon.

There were no troublesome memories in his childish sleep; no token came to him of his brave days at college, of the glittering years when he flustered the hearts of many girls. There were only the white, safe walls of his crib and Nana and a man who came to see him sometimes, and a great big orange ball that Nana pointed at just before his twilight bed hour and called "sun." When the sun went his eyes were sleepy—there were no dreams, no dreams to haunt him.

The past—the wild charge at the head of his men up San Juan Hill; the first years of his marriage when he worked late into the summer dusk down in the busy city for young Hildegarde whom he loved; the days before that when he sat smoking far into the night in the gloomy old Button house on Monroe Street with his grandfather-all these had faded like unsubstantial dreams from his mind as though they had never been. He did not remember.

He did not remember clearly whether the milk was warm or cool at his last feeding or how the days passed—there was only his crib and Nana's familiar presence. And then he remembered nothing. When he was hungry he cried—that was all. Through the noons and nights he breathed and over him there were soft mumblings and murmurings that he scarcely heard, and faintly differentiated smells, and light and darkness.

Then it was all dark, and his white crib and the dim faces that moved above him, and the warm sweet aroma of the milk, faded out altogether from his mind.

THE ADJUSTER

First published in
The Redbook Magazine, September, 1925

I

At five o'clock the sombre egg-shaped room at the Ritz ripens to a subtle melody—the light *clat-clat* of one lump, two lumps, into the cup, and the *ding* of the shining teapots and cream-pots as they kiss elegantly in transit upon a silver tray. There are those who cherish that amber hour above all other hours, for now the pale, pleasant toil of the lilies who inhabit the Ritz is over—the singing decorative part of the day remains.

Moving your eyes around the slightly raised horseshoe balcony you might, one spring afternoon, have seen young Mrs. Alphonse Karr and young Mrs. Charles Hemple at a table for two. The one in the dress was Mrs. Hemple—when I say "the dress" I refer to that black immaculate affair with the big buttons and the red ghost of a cape at the shoulders, a gown suggesting with faint and fashionable irreverence the garb of a French cardinal, as it was meant to do when it was invented in the Rue de la Paix. Mrs. Karr and Mrs. Hemple were twenty-three years old, and their enemies said that they had done very well for themselves. Either might have had her limousine waiting at the hotel door, but both of them much preferred to walk home (up Park Avenue) through the April twilight.

Luella Hemple was tall, with the sort of flaxen hair that English country girls should have, but seldom do. Her skin was radiant, and there was no need of putting anything on it at all, but in deference to an antiquated fashion—this was the year 1920—she had powdered out its high roses and drawn on it a new mouth and new eyebrows—which were no more successful than such meddling deserves. This, of course, is said from the vantage-point of 1925. In those days the effect she gave was exactly right.

"I've been married three years," she was saying as she squashed out a cigarette in an exhausted lemon. "The baby will be two years old to-morrow. I must remember to get——"

She took a gold pencil from her case and wrote "Candies" and "Things you pull, with paper caps," on an ivory date-pad. Then, raising her eyes, she looked at Mrs. Karr and hesitated.

"Shall I tell you something outrageous?"

"Try," said Mrs. Karr cheerfully.

"Even my baby bores me. That sounds unnatural, Ede, but it's true. He doesn't *begin* to fill my life. I love him with all my heart, but when I have him to take care of for an afternoon, I get so nervous that I want to scream. After two hours I begin praying for the moment the nurse'll walk in the door."

When she had made this confession, Luella breathed quickly and looked closely at her friend. She didn't really feel unnatural at all. This was the truth. There couldn't be anything vicious in the truth.

"It may be because you don't love Charles," ventured Mrs. Karr, unmoved.

"But I do! I hope I haven't given you that impression with all this talk." She decided that Ede Karr was stupid. "It's the very fact that I do love Charles that complicates matters. I cried myself to sleep last night because I know we're drifting slowly but surely toward a divorce. It's the baby that keeps us together."

Ede Karr, who had been married five years, looked at her critically to see if this was a pose, but Luella's lovely eyes were grave and sad.

"And what is the trouble?" Ede inquired.

"It's plural," said Luella, frowning. "First, there's food. I'm a vile housekeeper, and I have no intention of turning into a good one. I hate to order groceries, and I hate to go into the kitchen and poke around to see if the ice-box is clean, and I hate to pretend to the servants that I'm interested in their work, when really I never want to hear about food until it comes on the table. You see, I never learned to cook, and consequently a kitchen is about as interesting to me as a—as a boiler-room. It's simply a machine that I don't understand. It's easy to say, 'Go to cooking school,' the way people do in books—but, Ede, in real life does anybody ever change into a model *Hausfrau*—unless they have to?"

"Go on," said Ede non-committally. "Tell me more."

"Well, as a result, the house is always in a riot. The servants leave every week. If they're young and incompetent, I can't train them, so we have to let them go. If they're experienced, they hate a house where a woman doesn't take an intense interest in the price of asparagus. So they leave—and half the time we eat at restaurants and hotels."

"I don't suppose Charles likes that."

"Hates it. In fact, he hates about everything that I like. He's lukewarm about the theatre, hates the opera, hates dancing, hates cocktail parties—sometimes I think he hates everything pleasant in the world. I sat home for a year or so. While Chuck was on the way, and while I was nursing him, I didn't mind. But this year I told Charles frankly that I was still young enough to want some fun. And since then we've been going out whether he wants to or not." She paused, brooding. "I'm so sorry for him I don't know what to do, Ede—but if we sat home, I'd just be sorry for myself. And to tell you another true thing, I'd rather that he'd be unhappy than me."

Luella was not so much stating a case as thinking aloud. She considered that she was being very fair. Before her marriage men had always told her that she was "a good sport," and she had tried to carry this fairness into her married life. So she always saw Charley's point of view as clearly as she saw her own.

If she had been a pioneer wife, she would probably have fought the fight side by side with her husband. But here in New York there wasn't any fight. They weren't struggling together to obtain a far-off peace and leisure—she had more of either than she could use. Luella, like several thousand other young wives in New York, honestly wanted something to do. If she had had a little more money and a little less love, she could have gone in for horses or for vagarious amour. Or if they had had a little less money, her surplus energy would have been absorbed by hope and even by effort. But the Charles Hemples were in between. They were of that enormous American class who wander over Europe every summer, sneering rather pathetically and wistfully at the customs and traditions and pastimes of other countries, because they have no customs or traditions or pastimes of their own. It is a class sprung yesterday from fathers and mothers who might just as well have lived two hundred years ago.

The tea-hour had turned abruptly into the before-dinner hour. Most of the tables had emptied until the room was dotted rather than crowded with shrill isolated voices and remote, surprising laughter—in one corner the waiters were already covering the tables with white for dinner.

"Charles and I are on each other's nerves." In the new silence Luella's voice rang out with startling clearness, and she lowered it precipitately. "Little things. He keeps rubbing his face with his hand—all the time, at table, at the theatre—even when he's in bed. It drives me wild, and when things like that begin to irritate you, it's nearly over." She broke off and, reaching backward, drew up a light fur around her neck. "I hope I haven't bored you, Ede. It's on my mind, because to-night tells the story. I made an engagement for to-night—an interesting engagement, a supper after the theatre to meet some Russians, singers or dancers or something, and Charles says he won't go. If he doesn't—then I'm going alone. And that's the end."

She put her elbows on the table suddenly and, bending her eyes down into her smooth gloves, began to cry, stubbornly and quietly. There was no one near to see, but Ede Karr wished that she had taken her gloves off. She would have reached out consolingly and touched her bare hand. But the gloves were a symbol of the difficulty of sympathizing with a woman to whom life had given so much. Ede wanted to say that it would "come out all right," that it wasn't "so bad as it seemed," but she said nothing. Her only reaction was impatience and distaste.

A waiter stepped near and laid a folded paper on the table, and Mrs. Karr reached for it.

"No, you mustn't," murmured Luella brokenly. "No, I invited *you*! I've got the money right here."

II

The Hemples' apartment—they owned it—was in one of those impersonal white palaces that are known by number instead of name. They had furnished it on their honeymoon, gone to England for the big pieces, to Florence for the bric-à-brac, and to Venice for the lace and sheer linen of the curtains and for the glass of many colors which littered the table when they entertained. Luella enjoyed choosing things on her honeymoon. It gave a purposeful air to the trip, and saved it from ever turning into the rather dismal wandering among big hotels and desolate ruins which European honeymoons are apt to be.

They returned, and life began. On the grand scale. Luella found herself a lady of substance. It amazed her sometimes that the specially created apartment and the specially created limousine were hers, just as indisputably as the mortgaged suburban bungalow out of *The Ladies' Home Journal* and the last year's car that fate might have given her instead. She was even more amazed when it all began to bore her. But it did. . . .

The evening was at seven when she turned out of the April dusk, let herself into the hall, and saw her husband waiting in the living-room before an open fire. She came in without a sound, closed the door noiselessly behind her, and stood watching him for a moment through the pleasant effective vista of the small *salon* which intervened. Charles Hemple was in the middle thirties, with a young serious face and distinguished iron-gray hair which would be white in ten years more. That and his deep-set, dark-gray eyes were his most noticeable features—women always thought his hair was romantic; most of the time Luella thought so too.

At this moment she found herself hating him a little, for she saw that he had raised his hand to his face and was rubbing it nervously over his chin and mouth. It gave him an air of unflattering abstraction, and sometimes even obscured his words, so that she was continually saying "What?" She had spoken about it several times, and he had apologized in a surprised way. But obviously he didn't realize how noticeable and how irritating it was, for he continued to do it. Things had now reached such a precarious state that Luella dreaded speaking of such matters any more—a certain sort of word might precipitate the imminent scene.

Luella tossed her gloves and purse abruptly on the table. Hearing the faint sound, her husband looked out toward the hall.

"Is that you, dear?"

"Yes, dear."

She went into the living-room, and walked into his arms and kissed him tensely. Charles Hemple responded with unusual formality, and then turned her slowly around so that she faced across the room.

"I've brought some one home to dinner."

She saw then that they were not alone, and her first feeling was of strong relief; the rigid expression on her face softened into a shy, charming smile as she held out her hand.

"This is Doctor Moon—this is my wife."

A man a little older than her husband, with a round, pale, slightly lined face, came forward to meet her.

"Good evening, Mrs. Hemple," he said. "I hope I'm not

interfering with any arrangement of yours."

"Oh, no," Luella cried quickly. "I'm delighted that you're coming to dinner. We're quite alone."

Simultaneously she thought of her engagement to-night, and wondered if this could be a clumsy trap of Charles' to keep her at home. If it were, he had chosen his bait badly. This man—a tired placidity radiated from him, from his face, from his heavy, leisurely voice, even from the three-year-old shine of his clothes.

Nevertheless, she excused herself and went into the kitchen to see what was planned for dinner. As usual they were trying a new pair of servants, the luncheon had been ill-cooked and ill-served—she would let them go to-morrow. She hoped Charles would talk to them—she hated to get rid of servants. Sometimes they wept, and sometimes they were insolent, but Charles had a way with him. And they were always afraid of a man.

The cooking on the stove, however, had a soothing savor. Luella gave instructions about "which china," and unlocked a bottle of precious chianti from the buffet. Then she went in to kiss young Chuck good night.

"Has he been good?" she demanded as he crawled enthusiastically into her arms.

"Very good," said the governess. "We went for a long walk over by Central Park."

"Well, aren't you a smart boy!" She kissed him ecstatically.

"And he put his foot into the fountain, so we had to come home in a taxi right away and change his little shoe and stocking."

"That's right. Here, wait a minute, *Chuck*!" Luella unclasped the great yellow beads from around her neck and handed them to him. "You mustn't break mama's beads." She turned to the nurse. "Put them on my dresser, will you, after he's asleep?"

She felt a certain compassion for her son as she went away—the small enclosed life he led, that all children led, except in big families. He was a dear little rose, except on the days when she took care of him. His face was the same shape as hers; she was thrilled sometimes, and formed new resolves about life when his heart beat against her own.

In her own pink and lovely bedroom, she confined her attentions to her face, which she washed and restored. Doctor Moon didn't deserve a change of dress, and Luella found herself oddly tired, though she had done very little all day. She returned to the living-room, and they went in to dinner.

"Such a nice house, Mrs. Hemple," said Doctor Moon impersonally; "and let me congratulate you on your fine little boy."

"Thanks. Coming from a doctor, that's a nice compliment." She hesitated. "Do you specialize in children?"

"I'm not a specialist at all," he said. "I'm about the last of my kind—a general practitioner."

"The last in New York, anyhow," remarked Charles. He had begun rubbing his face nervously, and Luella fixed her eyes on Doctor Moon so that she wouldn't see. But at Charles's next words she looked back at him sharply.

"In fact," he said unexpectedly, "I've invited Doctor Moon here because I wanted you to have a talk with him to-night."

Luella sat up straight in her chair.

"A talk with *me*?"

"Doctor Moon's an old friend of mine, and I think he can tell you a few things, Luella, that you ought to know."

"Why—" She tried to laugh, but she was surprised and annoyed. "I don't see, exactly, what you mean. There's nothing the matter with me. I don't believe I've ever felt better in my life."

Doctor Moon looked at Charles, asking permission to speak. Charles nodded, and his hand went up automatically to his face.

"Your husband has told me a great deal about your unsatisfactory life together," said Doctor Moon, still impersonally. "He wonders if I can be of any help in smoothing things out."

Luella's face was burning.

"I have no particular faith in psychoanalysis," she said coldly, "and I scarcely consider myself a subject for it."

"Neither have I," answered Doctor Moon, apparently unconscious of the snub; "I have no particular faith in anything but myself. I told you I am not a specialist, nor, I may add, a faddist of any sort. I promise nothing."

For a moment Luella considered leaving the room. But the effrontery of the suggestion aroused her curiosity too.

"I can't imagine what Charles has told you," she said, controlling herself with difficulty, "much less why. But I assure you that our affairs are a matter entirely between my husband and me. If you have no objections, Doctor Moon, I'd much prefer to discuss something—less personal."

Doctor Moon nodded heavily and politely. He made no further attempt to open the subject, and dinner proceeded in what was little more than a defeated silence. Luella determined that, whatever happened, she would adhere to her plans for to-night. An hour ago her independence had demanded it, but now some gesture of defiance had become necessary to her self-respect. She would stay in the living-room for a short moment after dinner; then, when the coffee came, she would excuse herself and dress to go out.

But when they did leave the dining-room, it was Charles who, in a quick, unarguable way, vanished.

"I have a letter to write," he said; "I'll be back in a moment." Before Luella could make a diplomatic objection, he went quickly down the corridor to his room, and she heard him shut his door.

Angry and confused, Luella poured the coffee and sank into a corner of the couch, looking intently at the fire.

"Don't be afraid, Mrs. Hemple," said Doctor Moon suddenly. "This was forced upon me. I do not act as a free agent——"

"I'm not afraid of you," she interrupted. But she knew that she was lying. She was a little afraid of him, if only for his dull insensitiveness to her distaste.

"Tell me about your trouble," he said very naturally, as though she were not a free agent either. He wasn't even looking at her, and except that they were alone in the room, he scarcely seemed to be addressing her at all.

The words that were in Luella's mind, her will, on her lips, were: "I'll do no such thing." What she actually said amazed her. It came out of her spontaneously, with apparently no co-operation of her own.

"Didn't you see him rubbing his face at dinner?" she said despairingly. "Are you blind? He's become so irritating to me that I think I'll go mad."

"I see." Doctor Moon's round face nodded.

"Don't you see I've had enough of home?" Her breasts seemed to struggle for air under her dress. "Don't you see how bored I am with keeping house, with the baby—everything seems as if it's going on forever and ever? I want excitement; and I don't care what form it takes or what I pay for it, so long as it makes my heart beat."

"I see."

It infuriated Luella that he claimed to understand. Her feeling of defiance had reached such a pitch that she preferred that no one should understand. She was content to be justified by the impassioned sincerity of her desires.

"I've tried to be good, and I'm not going to try any more. If I'm one of those women who wreck their lives for nothing, then I'll do it now. You can call me selfish, or silly, and be quite right; but in five minutes I'm going out of this house and begin to be alive."

This time Doctor Moon didn't answer, but he raised his head as if he were listening to something that was taking place a little distance away.

"You're not going out," he said after a moment; "I'm quite sure you're not going out."

Luella laughed.

"I *am* going out."

He disregarded this.

"You see, Mrs. Hemple, your husband isn't well. He's been trying to live your kind of life, and the strain of it has been too much for him. When he rubs his mouth——"

Light steps came down the corridor, and the maid, with a frightened expression on her face, tiptoed into the room.

"Mrs. Hemple——"

Startled at the interruption, Luella turned quickly.

"Yes?"

"Can I speak to—?" Her fear broke precipitately through her slight training. "Mr. Hemple, he's sick! He came into the kitchen a while ago and began throwing all the food out of the ice-box, and now he's in his room, crying and singing——"

Suddenly Luella heard his voice.

III

Charles Hemple had had a nervous collapse. There were twenty years of almost uninterrupted toil upon his shoulders, and the recent pressure at home had been too much for him to bear. His attitude toward his wife was the weak point in what had otherwise been a strong-minded and well-organized career—he was aware of her intense selfishness, but it is one of the many flaws in the scheme of human relationships that selfishness in women has an irresistible appeal to many men. Luella's selfishness existed side by side with a childish beauty, and, in consequence, Charles Hemple had begun to take the blame upon himself for situations which she had obviously brought about. It was an unhealthy attitude, and his mind had sickened, at length, with his attempts to put himself in the wrong.

After the first shock and the momentary flush of pity that followed it, Luella looked at the situation with impatience. She was "a good sport"—she couldn't take advantage of Charles when he was sick. The question of her liberties had to be postponed until he was on his feet. Just when she had determined to be a wife no longer, Luella was compelled to be a nurse as well. She sat beside his bed while he talked about her in his delirium—about the days of their engagement, and how some friend had told him then that he was making a mistake, and about his happiness in the early months of their marriage, and his growing disquiet as the gap appeared. Evidently he had been more aware of it than she had thought—more than he ever said.

"Luella!" He would lurch up in bed. "Luella! Where *are* you?"

"I'm right here, Charles, beside you." She tried to make her voice cheerful and warm.

"If you want to go, Luella, you'd better go. I don't seem to be enough for you any more."

She denied this soothingly.

"I've thought it over, Luella, and I can't ruin my health on account of you—" Then quickly, and passionately: "Don't go, Luella, for God's sake, don't go away and leave me! Promise me you won't! I'll do anything you say if you won't go."

His humility annoyed her most; he was a reserved man, and she had never guessed at the extent of his devotion before.

"I'm only going for a minute. It's Doctor Moon, your friend, Charles. He came to-day to see how you were, don't you remember? And he wants to talk to me before he goes."

"You'll come back?" he persisted.

"In just a little while. There—lie quiet."

She raised his head and plumped his pillow into freshness. A new trained nurse would arrive to-morrow.

In the living-room Doctor Moon was waiting—his suit more worn and shabby in the afternoon light. She disliked him inordinately, with an illogical conviction that he was in some way to blame for her misfortune, but he was so deeply interested that she couldn't refuse to see him. She hadn't asked him to consult with the specialists, though—a doctor who was so down at the heel. . . .

"Mrs. Hemple." He came forward, holding out his hand, and Luella touched it, lightly and uneasily.

"You seem well," he said.

"I am well, thank you."

"I congratulate you on the way you've taken hold of things."

"But I haven't taken hold of things at all," she said coldly. "I do what I have to——"

"That's just it."

Her impatience mounted rapidly.

"I do what I have to, and nothing more," she continued; "and with no particular good-will."

Suddenly she opened up to him again, as she had the night of the catastrophe—realizing that she was putting herself on a footing of intimacy with him, yet unable to restrain her words.

"The house isn't going," she broke out bitterly. "I had to discharge the servants, and now I've got a woman in by the day. And the baby has a cold, and I've found out that his nurse doesn't know her business, and everything's just as messy and terrible as it can be!"

"Would you mind telling me how you found out the nurse didn't know her business?"

"You find out various unpleasant things when you're forced to stay around the house."

He nodded, his weary face turning here and there about the room.

"I feel somewhat encouraged," he said slowly. "As I told you, I promise nothing; I only do the best I can."

Luella looked up at him, startled.

"What do you mean?" she protested. "You've done nothing for me—nothing at all!"

"Nothing much—yet," he said heavily. "It takes time, Mrs. Hemple."

The words were said in a dry monotone that was somehow without offense, but Luella felt that he had gone too far. She got to her feet.

"I've met your type before," she said coldly. "For some reason you seem to think that you have a standing here as 'the old friend of the family.' But I don't make friends quickly, and I haven't given you the privilege of being so"—she wanted to say "insolent," but the word eluded her—"so personal with me."

When the front door had closed behind him, Luella went into the kitchen to see if the woman understood about the three different dinners—one for Charles, one for the baby, and one for herself. It was hard to do with only a single servant when things were so complicated. She must try another employment agency—this one had begun to sound bored.

To her surprise, she found the cook with hat and coat on, reading a newspaper at the kitchen table.

"Why"—Luella tried to think of the name—"why, what's the matter, Mrs.——"

"Mrs. Danski is my name."

"What's the matter?"

"I'm afraid I won't be able to accommodate you," said Mrs. Danski. "You see, I'm only a plain cook, and I'm not used to preparing invalid's food."

"But I've counted on you."

"I'm very sorry." She shook her head stubbornly. "I've got my own health to think of. I'm sure they didn't tell me what kind of a job it was when I came. And when you asked me to clean out your husband's room, I knew it was way beyond my powers."

"I won't ask you to clean anything," said Luella desperately. "If you'll just stay until to-morrow. I can't possibly get anybody else to-night."

Mrs. Danski smiled politely.

"I got my own children to think of, just like you."

It was on Luella's tongue to offer her more money, but suddenly her temper gave way.

"I've never heard of anything so selfish in my life!" she broke out. "To leave me at a time like this! You're an old fool!"

"If you'd pay me for my time, I'd go," said Mrs. Danski calmly.

"I won't pay you a cent unless you'll stay!"

She was immediately sorry she had said this, but she was too proud to withdraw the threat.

"You will so pay me!"

"You go out that door!"

"I'll go when I get my money," asserted Mrs. Danski indignantly. "I got my children to think of."

Luella drew in her breath sharply, and took a step forward. Intimidated by her intensity, Mrs. Danski turned and flounced, muttering, out of the door.

Luella went to the phone and, calling up the agency, explained that the woman had left.

"Can you send me some one right away? My husband is sick and the baby's sick——"

"I'm sorry, Mrs. Hemple; there's no one in the office now. It's after four o'clock."

Luella argued for a while. Finally she obtained a promise that they would telephone to an emergency woman they knew. That was the best they could do until to-morrow.

She called several other agencies, but the servant industry had apparently ceased to function for the day. After giving Charles his medicine, she tiptoed softly into the nursery.

"How's baby?" she asked abstractedly.

"Ninety-nine one," whispered the nurse, holding the thermometer to the light. "I just took it."

"Is that much?" asked Luella, frowning.

"It's just three-fifths of a degree. That isn't so much for the afternoon. They often run up a little with a cold."

Luella went over to the cot and laid her hand on her son's flushed cheek, thinking, in the midst of her anxiety, how much he resembled the incredible cherub of the "Lux" advertisement in the bus.

She turned to the nurse.

"Do you know how to cook?"

"Why—I'm not a good cook."

"Well, can you do the baby's food to-night? That old fool has left, and I can't get anyone, and I don't know what to do."

"Oh, yes, I can do the baby's food."

"That's all right, then. I'll try to fix something for Mr. Hemple. Please have your door open so you can hear the bell when the doctor comes. And let me know."

So many doctors! There had scarcely been an hour all day when there wasn't a doctor in the house. The specialist and their family physician every morning, then the baby doctor—and this afternoon there had been Doctor Moon, placid, persistent, unwelcome, in the parlor. Luella went into the kitchen. She could cook bacon and eggs for herself—she had often done that after the theatre. But the vegetables for Charles were a different matter—they must be left to boil or stew or something, and the stove had so many doors and ovens that she couldn't decide which to use. She chose a blue pan that looked new, sliced carrots into it, and covered them with a little water. As she put it on the stove and tried to remember what to do next, the phone rang. It was the agency.

"Yes, this is Mrs. Hemple speaking."

"Why, the woman we sent to you has returned here with the claim that you refused to pay her for her time."

"I explained to you that she refused to stay," said Luella hotly. "She didn't keep her agreement, and I didn't feel I was under any obligation——"

"We have to see that our people are paid," the agency informed her; "otherwise we wouldn't be helping them at all, would we? I'm sorry, Mrs. Hemple, but we won't be able to furnish you with any one else until this little matter is arranged."

"Oh, I'll pay, I'll pay!" she cried.

"Of course we like to keep on good terms with our clients——"

"Yes—yes!"

"So if you'll send her money around to-morrow? It's seventy-five cents an hour."

"But how about to-night?" she exclaimed. "I've got to have some one to-night."

"Why—it's pretty late now. I was just going home myself."

"But I'm Mrs. Charles Hemple! Don't you understand? I'm perfectly good for what I say I'll do. I'm the wife of Charles Hemple, of 14 Broadway——"

Simultaneously she realized that Charles Hemple of 14 Broadway was a helpless invalid—he was neither a reference nor a refuge any more. In despair at the sudden callousness of the world, she hung up the receiver.

After another ten minutes of frantic muddling in the kitchen, she went to the baby's nurse, whom she disliked, and confessed that she was unable to cook her husband's dinner. The nurse announced that she had a splitting headache, and that with a sick child her hands were full already, but she consented, without enthusiasm, to show Luella what to do.

Swallowing her humiliation, Luella obeyed orders while the nurse experimented, grumbling, with the unfamiliar stove. Dinner was started after a fashion. Then it was time for the nurse to bathe Chuck, and Luella sat down alone at the kitchen table, and listened to the bubbling perfume that escaped from the pans.

"And women do this every day," she thought.

"Thousands of women. Cook and take care of sick people—and go out to work too."

But she didn't think of those women as being like her, except in the superficial aspect of having two feet and two hands. She said it as she might have said "South Sea Islanders wear nose-rings." She was merely slumming to-day in her own home, and she wasn't enjoying it. For her, it was merely a ridiculous exception.

Suddenly she became aware of slow approaching steps in the dining-room and then in the butler's pantry. Half afraid that it was Doctor Moon coming to pay another call, she looked up—and saw the nurse coming through the pantry door. It flashed through Luella's mind that the nurse was going to be sick too. And she was right—the nurse had hardly reached the kitchen door when she lurched and clutched at the handle as a winged bird clings to a branch. Then she receded wordlessly to the floor. Simultaneously the door-bell rang; and Luella, getting to her feet, gasped with relief that the baby doctor had come.

"Fainted, that's all," he said, taking the girl's head into his lap.

The eyes fluttered. "Yep, she fainted, that's all."

"Everybody's sick!" cried Luella with a sort of despairing humor. "Everybody's sick but me, doctor."

"This one's not sick," he said after a moment. "Her heart is normal already. She just fainted."

When she had helped the doctor raise the quickening body to a chair, Luella hurried into the nursery and bent over the baby's bed. She let down one of the iron sides quietly. The fever seemed to be gone now—the flush had faded away. She bent over to touch the small cheek.

Suddenly Luella began to scream.

IV

Even after her baby's funeral, Luella still couldn't believe that she had lost him. She came back to the apartment and walked around the nursery in a circle, saying his name. Then, frightened by grief, she sat down and stared at his white rocker with the red chicken painted on the side.

"What will become of me now?" she whispered to herself. "Something awful is going to happen to me when I realize that I'll never see Chuck any more!"

She wasn't sure yet. If she waited here till twilight, the nurse might still bring him in from his walk. She remembered a tragic confusion in the midst of which some one had told her that Chuck was dead, but if that was so, then why was his room waiting, with his small brush and comb still on the bureau, and why was she here at all?

"Mrs. Hemple."

She looked up. The weary, shabby figure of Doctor Moon stood in the door.

"You go away," Luella said dully.

"Your husband needs you."

"I don't care."

Doctor Moon came a little way into the room.

"I don't think you understand, Mrs. Hemple. He's been calling for you. You haven't any one now except him."

"I hate you," she said suddenly.

"If you like. I promised nothing, you know. I do the best I can. You'll be better when you realize that your baby is gone, that you're not going to see him any more."

Luella sprang to her feet.

"My baby isn't dead!" she cried. "You lie! You always lie!" Her flashing eyes looked into his and caught something there, at once brutal and kind, that awed her and made her impotent and acquiescent. She lowered her own eyes in tired despair.

"All right," she said wearily. "My baby is gone. What shall I do now?"

"Your husband is much better. All he needs is rest and kindness. But you must go to him and tell him what's happened."

"I suppose you think you made him better," said Luella bitterly.

"Perhaps. He's nearly well."

Nearly well—then the last link that held her to her home was broken. This part of her life was over—she could cut it off here, with its grief and oppression, and be off now, free as the wind.

"I'll go to him in a minute," Luella said in a faraway voice. "Please leave me alone."

Doctor Moon's unwelcome shadow melted into the darkness of the hall.

"I can go away," Luella whispered to herself. "Life has given me back freedom, in place of what it took away from me."

But she mustn't linger even a minute, or Life would bind her again and make her suffer once more. She called the apartment porter and asked that her trunk be brought up from the storeroom. Then she began taking things from the bureau and wardrobe, trying to approximate as nearly as possible the possessions that she had brought to her married life. She even found two old dresses that had formed part of her trousseau—

out of style now, and a little tight in the hips—which she threw in with the rest. A new life. Charles was well again; and her baby, whom she had worshipped, and who had bored her a little, was dead.

When she had packed her trunk, she went into the kitchen automatically, to see about the preparations for dinner. She spoke to the cook about the special things for Charles and said that she herself was dining out. The sight of one of the small pans that had been used to cook Chuck's food caught her attention for a moment—but she stared at it unmoved. She looked into the ice-box and saw it was clean and fresh inside. Then she went into Charles's room. He was sitting up in bed, and the nurse was reading to him. His hair was almost white now, silvery white, and underneath it his eyes were huge and dark in his thin young face.

"The baby is sick?" he asked in his own natural voice.

She nodded.

He hesitated, closing his eyes for a moment. Then he asked:

"The baby is dead?"

"Yes."

For a long time he didn't speak. The nurse came over and put her hand on his forehead. Two large, strange tears welled from his eyes.

"I knew the baby was dead."

After another long wait, the nurse spoke:

"The doctor said he could be taken out for a drive to-day while there was still sunshine. He needs a little change."

"Yes."

"I thought"—the nurse hesitated—"I thought perhaps it would do you both good, Mrs. Hemple, if you took him instead of me."

Luella shook her head hastily.

"Oh, no," she said. "I don't feel able to, to-day."

The nurse looked at her oddly. With a sudden feeling of pity for Charles, Luella bent down gently and kissed his cheek. Then, without a word, she went to her own room, put on her hat and coat, and with her suitcase started for the front door.

Immediately she saw that there was a shadow in the hall. If she could get past that shadow, she was free. If she could go to the right or left of it, or order it out of her way! But, stubbornly, it refused to move, and with a little cry she sank down into a hall chair.

"I thought you'd gone," she wailed. "I told you to go away."

"I'm going soon," said Doctor Moon, "but I don't want you to make an old mistake."

"I'm not making a mistake—I'm leaving my mistakes behind."

"You're trying to leave yourself behind, but you can't. The more you try to run away from yourself, the more you'll have yourself with you."

"But I've got to go away," she insisted wildly. "Out of this house of death and failure!"

"You haven't failed yet. You've only begun."

She stood up.

"Let me pass."

"No."

Abruptly she gave way, as she always did when he talked to her. She covered her face with her hands and burst into tears.

"Go back into that room and tell the nurse you'll take your husband for a drive," he suggested.

"I can't."

"Oh, yes."

Once more Luella looked at him, and knew that she would obey. With the conviction that her spirit was broken at last, she took up her suitcase and walked back through the hall.

V

The nature of the curious influence that Doctor Moon exerted upon her, Luella could not guess. But as the days passed, she found herself doing many things that had been repugnant

165

to her before. She stayed at home with Charles; and when he grew better, she went out with him sometimes to dinner, or the theatre, but only when he expressed a wish. She visited the kitchen every day, and kept an unwilling eye on the house, at first with a horror that it would go wrong again, then from habit. And she felt that it was all somehow mixed up with Doctor Moon—it was something he kept telling her about life, or almost telling her, and yet concealing from her, as though he were afraid to have her know.

With the resumption of their normal life, she found that Charles was less nervous. His habit of rubbing his face had left him, and if the world seemed less gay and happy to her than it had before, she experienced a certain peace, sometimes, that she had never known.

Then, one afternoon, Doctor Moon told her suddenly that he was going away.

"Do you mean for good?" she demanded with a touch of panic.

"For good."

For a strange moment she wasn't sure whether she was glad or sorry.

"You don't need me any more," he said quietly. "You don't realize it, but you've grown up."

He came over and, sitting on the couch beside her, took her hand.

Luella sat silent and tense—listening.

"We make an agreement with children that they can sit in the audience without helping to make the play," he said, "but if they still sit in the audience after they're grown, somebody's got to work double time for them, so that they can enjoy the light and glitter of the world."

"But I want the light and glitter," she protested. "That's all there is in life. There can't be anything wrong in wanting to have things warm."

"Things will still be warm."

"How?"

"Things will warm themselves from you."

Luella looked at him, startled.

"It's your turn to be the centre, to give others what was given to you for so long. You've got to give security to young people and peace to your husband, and a sort of charity to the old. You've got to let the people who work for you depend on you. You've got to cover up a few more troubles than you show, and be a little more patient than the average person, and do a little more instead of a little less than your share. The light and glitter of the world is in your hands."

He broke off suddenly.

"Get up," he said, "and go to that mirror and tell me what you see."

Obediently Luella got up and went close to a purchase of her honeymoon, a Venetian pier-glass on the wall.

"I see new lines in my face here," she said, raising her finger and placing it between her eyes, "and a few shadows at the sides that might be—that are little wrinkles."

"Do you care?"

She turned quickly. "No," she said.

"Do you realize that Chuck is gone? That you'll never see him any more?"

"Yes." She passed her hands slowly over her eyes. "But that all seems so vague and far away."

"Vague and far away," he repeated; and then: "And are you afraid of me now?"

"Not any longer," she said, and she added frankly, "now that you're going away."

He moved toward the door. He seemed particularly weary to-night, as though he could hardly move about at all.

"The household here is in your keeping," he said in a tired whisper. "If there is any light and warmth in it, it will be your light and warmth; if it is happy, it will be because you've made it so. Happy things may come to you in life, but you must never go seeking them any more. It is your turn to make the fire."

"Won't you sit down a moment longer?" Luella ventured.

"There isn't time." His voice was so low now that she could scarcely hear the words. "But remember that whatever suffering comes to you, I can always help you—if it is something that can be helped. I promise nothing."

He opened the door. She must find out now what she most wanted to know, before it was too late.

"What have you done to me?" she cried. "Why have I no sorrow left for Chuck—for anything at all? Tell me; I almost see, yet I can't see. Before you go—tell me who you are!"

"Who am I?—" His worn suit paused in the doorway. His round, pale face seemed to dissolve into two faces, a dozen faces, a score, each one different yet the same—sad, happy, tragic, indiffrent, resigned—until threescore Doctor Moons were ranged like an infinite series of reflections, like months stretching into the vista of the past.

"Who am I?" he repeated; "I am five years."

The door closed.

* * * * *

At six o'clock Charles Hemple came home, and as usual Luella met him in the hall. Except that now his hair was dead white, his long illness of two years had left no mark upon him. Luella herself was more noticeably changed—she was a little stouter, and there were those fines around her eyes that had come when Chuck died one evening back in 1921. But she was still lovely, and there was a mature kindness about her face at twenty-eight, as if suffering had touched her only reluctantly and then hurried away.

"Ede and her husband are coming to dinner," she said. "I've got theatre tickets, but if you're tired, I don't care whether we go or not."

"I'd like to go."

She looked at him.

"You wouldn't."

"I really would."

"We'll see how you feel after dinner."

He put his arm around her waist. Together they walked into the nursery where the two children were waiting up to say good night.

RAGS MARTIN-JONES
AND THE PR-NCE OF W-LES

First published in
McCall's, July, 1926

I

The *Majestic* came gliding into New York harbor on an April morning. She sniffed at the tugboats and turtle-gaited ferries, winked at a gaudy young yacht, and ordered a cattle-boat out of her way with a snarling whistle of steam. Then she parked at her private dock with all the fuss of a stout lady sitting down, and announced complacently that she had just come from Cherbourg and Southampton with a cargo of the very best people in the world.

The very best people in the world stood on the deck and waved idiotically to their poor relations who were waiting on the dock for gloves from Paris. Before long a great toboggan had connected the *Majestic* with the North American continent, and the ship began to disgorge these very best people in the world—who turned out to be Gloria Swanson, two buyers from Lord & Taylor, the financial minister from Graustark with a proposal for funding the debt, and an African king who had been trying to land somewhere all winter and was feeling violently sea-sick.

The photographers worked passionately as the stream of passengers flowed on to the dock. There was a burst of cheering at the appearance of a pair of stretchers laden with two Middle-Westerners who had drunk themselves delirious on the last night out.

The deck gradually emptied, but when the last bottle of Benedictine had reached shore the photographers still remained at their posts. And the officer in charge of debarkation still stood at the foot of the gangway, glancing first at his watch and then at the deck as if some important part of the cargo was still on board. At last from the watchers on the pier there arose a long-drawn "Ah-h-h!" as a final entourage began to stream down from deck B.

First came two French maids, carrying small, purple dogs, and followed by a squad of porters, blind and invisible under innumerable bunches and bouquets of fresh flowers. Another maid followed, leading a sad-eyed orphan child of a French flavor, and close upon its heels walked the second officer pulling along three neurasthenic wolfhounds, much to their reluctance and his own.

A pause. Then the captain, Sir Howard George Witchcraft, appeared at the rail, with something that might have been a pile of gorgeous silver-fox fur standing by his side.

Rags Martin-Jones, after five years in the capitals of Europe, was returning to her native land!

Rags Martin-Jones was not a dog. She was half a girl and half a flower, and as she shook hands with Captain Sir Howard George Witchcraft she smiled as if some one had told her the newest, freshest joke in the world. All the people who had not already left the pier felt that smile trembling on the April air and turned around to see.

She came slowly down the gangway. Her hat, an expensive, inscrutable experiment, was crushed under her arm, so that her scant boy's hair, convict's hair, tried unsuccessfully to toss and flop a little in the harbor wind. Her face was like seven o'clock on a wedding morning save where she had slipped a preposterous monocle into an eye of clear childish blue. At every few steps her long lashes would tilt out the monocle, and she would laugh, a bored, happy laugh, and replace the supercilious spectacle in the other eye.

Tap! Her one hundred and five pounds reached the pier and it seemed to sway and bend from the shock of her beauty. A few porters fainted. A large, sentimental shark which had followed the ship across made a despairing leap to see her once more, and then dove, broken-hearted, back into the deep sea. Rags Martin-Jones had come home.

There was no member of her family there to meet her, for the simple reason that she was the only member of her family left alive. In 1913 her parents had gone down on the *Titanic* together rather than be separated in this world, and so the Martin-Jones fortune of seventy-five millions had been inherited by a very little girl on her tenth birthday. It was what the consumer always refers to as a "shame."

Rags Martin-Jones (everybody had forgotten her real name long ago) was now photographed from all sides. The monocle persistently fell out, and she kept laughing and yawning and replacing it, so no very clear picture of her was taken—except by the motion-picture camera. All the photographs, however, included a flustered, handsome young man, with an almost ferocious love-light burning in his eyes, who had met her on the dock. His name was John M. Chestnut, he had already written the story of his success for the *American Magazine*, and he had been hopelessly in love with Rags ever since the time when she, like the tides, had come under the influence of the summer moon.

When Rags became really aware of his presence they were walking down the pier, and she looked at him blankly as though she had never seen him before in this world.

"Rags," he began, "Rags——"

"John M. Chestnut?" she inquired, inspecting him with great interest.

"Of course!" he exclaimed angrily. "Are you trying to pretend you don't know me? That you didn't write me to meet you here?"

She laughed. A chauffeur appeared at her elbow, and she

twisted out of her coat, revealing a dress made in great splashy checks of sea-blue and gray. She shook herself like a wet bird.

"I've got a lot of junk to declare," she remarked absently.

"So have I," said Chestnut anxiously, "and the first thing I want to declare is that I've loved you, Rags, every minute since you've been away."

She stopped him with a groan.

"Please! There were some young Americans on the boat. The subject has become a bore."

"My God!" cried Chestnut, "do you mean to say that you class *my* love with what was said to you on a *boat*?"

His voice had risen, and several people in the vicinity turned to hear.

"Sh!" she warned him, "I'm not giving a circus. If you want me to even see you while I'm here, you'll have to be less violent."

But John M. Chestnut seemed unable to control his voice.

"Do you mean to say"—it trembled to a carrying pitch—"that you've forgotten what you said on this very pier five years ago last Thursday?"

Half the passengers from the ship were now watching the scene on the dock, and another little eddy drifted out of the customs-house to see.

"John"—her displeasure was increasing—"if you raise your voice again I'll arrange it so you'll have plenty of chance to cool off. I'm going to the Ritz. Come and see me there this afternoon."

"But, Rags!" he protested hoarsely. "Listen to me. Five years ago——"

Then the watchers on the dock were treated to a curious sight. A beautiful lady in a checkered dress of sea-blue and gray took a brisk step forward so that her hands came into contact with an excited young man by her side. The young man retreating instinctively reached back with his foot, but, finding nothing, relapsed gently off the thirty-foot dock and plopped, after a not ungraceful revolution, into the Hudson River.

A shout of alarm went up, and there was a rush to the edge

just as his head appeared above water. He was swimming easily, and, perceiving this, the young lady who had apparently been the cause of the accident leaned over the pier and made a megaphone of her hands.

"I'll be in at half past four," she cried.

And with a cheerful wave of her hand, which the engulfed gentleman was unable to return, she adjusted her monocle, threw one haughty glance at the gathered crowd, and walked leisurely from the scene.

II

The five dogs, the three maids, and the French orphan were installed in the largest suite at the Ritz, and Rags tumbled lazily into a steaming bath, fragrant with herbs, where she dozed for the greater part of an hour. At the end of that time she received business calls from a masseuse, a manicure, and finally a Parisian hair-dresser, who restored her hair-cut to criminal's length. When John M. Chestnut arrived at four he found half a dozen lawyers and bankers, the administrators of the Martin-Jones trust fund, waiting in the hall. They had been there since half past one, and were now in a state of considerable agitation.

After one of the maids had subjected him to a severe scrutiny, possibly to be sure that he was thoroughly dry, John was conducted immediately into the presence of m'selle. M'selle was in her bedroom reclining on the chaise-longue among two dozen silk pillows that had accompanied her from the other side. John came into the room somewhat stiffly and greeted her with a formal bow.

"You look better," she said, raising herself from her pillows and staring at him appraisingly. "It gave you a color."

He thanked her coldly for the compliment.

"You ought to go in every morning." And then she added irrelevantly: "I'm going back to Paris to-morrow."

John Chestnut gasped.

"I wrote you that I didn't intend to stay more than a week anyhow," she added.

"But, Rags——"

"Why should I? There isn't an amusing man in New York."

"But listen, Rags, won't you give me a chance? Won't you stay for, say, ten days and get to know me a little?"

"Know you!" Her tone implied that he was already a far too open book. "I want a man who's capable of a gallant gesture."

"Do you mean you want me to express myself entirely in pantomime?"

Rags uttered a disgusted sigh.

"I mean you haven't any imagination," she explained patiently. "No Americans have any imagination. Paris is the only large city where a civilized woman can breathe."

"Don't you care for me at all any more?"

"I wouldn't have crossed the Atlantic to see you if I didn't. But as soon as I looked over the Americans on the boat, I knew I couldn't marry one. I'd just hate you, John, and the only fun I'd have out of it would be the fun of breaking your heart."

She began to twist herself down among the cushions until she almost disappeared from view.

"I've lost my monocle," she explained.

After an unsuccessful search in the silken depths she discovered the illusive glass hanging down the back of her neck.

"I'd love to be in love," she went on, replacing the monocle in her childish eye. "Last spring in Sorrento I almost eloped with an Indian rajah, but he was half a shade too dark, and I took an intense dislike to one of his other wives."

"Don't talk that rubbish!" cried John, sinking his face into his hands.

"Well, I didn't marry him," she protested. "But in one way he had a lot to offer. He was the third richest subject of the British Empire. That's another thing—are you rich?"

"Not as rich as you."

"There you are. What have you to offer me?"

"Love."

"Love!" She disappeared again among the cushions. "Listen, John. Life to me is a series of glistening bazaars with a merchant in front of each one rubbing his hands together and saying 'Patronize this place here. Best bazaar in the world.' So I go in with my purse full of beauty and money and youth, all prepared to buy. 'What have you got for sale?' I ask him, and he rubs his hands together and says: 'Well, Mademoiselle, to-day we have some perfectly be-*oo* tiful love.' Sometimes he hasn't even got that in stock, but he sends out for it when he finds I have so much money to spend. Oh, he always gives me love before I go— and for nothing. That's the one revenge I have."

John Chestnut rose despairingly to his feet and took a step toward the window.

"Don't throw yourself out," Rags exclaimed quickly.

"All right." He tossed his cigarette down into Madison Avenue.

"It isn't just you," she said in a softer voice. "Dull and uninspired as you are, I care for you more than I can say. But life's so endless here. Nothing ever comes off."

"Loads of things come off," he insisted. "Why, to-day there was an intellectual murder in Hoboken and a suicide by proxy in Maine. A bill to sterilize agnostics is before Congress——"

"I have no interest in humor," she objected, "but I have an almost archaic predilection for romance. Why, John, last month I sat at a dinner-table while two men flipped a coin for the kingdom of Schwartzberg-Rhineminster. In Paris I knew a man named Blutchdak who really started the war, and has a new one planned for year after next."

"Well, just for a rest you come out with me to-night," he said doggedly.

"Where to?" demanded Rags with scorn. "Do you think I still thrill at a night-club and a bottle of sugary mousseaux? I prefer my own gaudy dreams."

"I'll take you to the most highly-strung place in the city."

"What'll happen? You've got to tell me what'll happen."

John Chestnut suddenly drew a long breath and looked cautiously around as if he were afraid of being overheard.

"Well, to tell you the truth," he said in a low, worried tone, "if everything was known, something pretty awful would be liable to happen to *me*."

She sat upright and the pillows tumbled about her like leaves.

"Do you mean to imply that there's anything shady in your life?" she cried, with laughter in her voice. "Do you expect me to believe that? No, John, you'll have your fun by plugging ahead on the beaten path—just plugging ahead."

Her mouth, a small insolent rose, dropped the words on him like thorns. John took his hat and coat from the chair and picked up his cane.

"For the last time—will you come along with me to-night and see what you will see?"

"See what? See who? Is there anything in this country worth seeing?"

"Well," he said, in a matter-of-fact tone, "for one thing you'll see the Prince of Wales."

"What?" She left the chaise-longue at a bound. "Is he back in New York?"

"He will be to-night. Would you care to see him?"

"Would I? I've never seen him. I've missed him everywhere. I'd give a year of my life to see him for an hour." Her voice trembled with excitement.

"He's been in Canada. He's down here incognito for the big prize-fight this afternoon. And I happen to know where he's going to be to-night."

Rags gave a sharp ecstatic cry:

"Dominic! Louise! Germaine!"

The three maids came running. The room filled suddenly with vibrations of wild, startled light.

"Dominic, the car!" cried Rags in French. "St. Raphael, my gold dress and the slippers with the real gold heels. The big pearls too—all the pearls, and the egg-diamond and the stockings with the sapphire clocks. Germaine—send for a beauty-parlor on the run. My bath again—ice cold and half full of almond cream. Dominic—Tiffany's, like lightning, before they close. Find me a brooch, a pendant, a tiara, anything—it doesn't matter—with the arms of the house of Windsor."

She was fumbling at the buttons of her dress—and as John turned quickly to go, it was already sliding from her shoulders.

"Orchids!" she called after him, "orchids, for the love of heaven! Four dozen, so I can choose four."

And then maids flew here and there about the room like frightened birds. "Perfume, St. Raphael, open the perfume trunk, and my rose-colored sables, and my diamond garters, and the sweet-oil for my hands! Here, take these things! This too—and this—ouch!—and this!"

With becoming modesty John Chestnut closed the outside door. The six trustees in various postures of fatigue, of ennui, of resignation, of despair, were still cluttering up the outer hall.

"Gentlemen," announced John Chestnut, "I fear that Miss Martin-Jones is much too weary from her trip to talk to you this afternoon."

III

"This place, for no particular reason, is called the Hole in the Sky."

Rags looked around her. They were on a roof-garden wide open to the April night. Overhead the true stars winked cold, and there was a lunar sliver of ice in the dark west. But where they stood it was warm as June, and the couples dining or dancing on the opaque glass floor were unconcerned with the forbidding sky.

"What makes it so warm?" she whispered as they moved toward a table.

"It's some new invention that keeps the warm air from rising. I don't know the principle of the thing, but I know that they can keep it open like this even in the middle of winter—"

"Where's the Prince of Wales?" she demanded tensely.

John looked around.

"He hasn't arrived yet. He won't be here for about half an hour."

She sighed profoundly.

"It's the first time I've been excited in four years."

Four years—one year less than he had loved her. He wondered if when she was sixteen, a wild lovely child, sitting up all night in restaurants with officers who were to leave for Brest next day, losing the glamour of life too soon in the old, sad, poignant days of the war, she had ever been so lovely as under these amber lights and this dark sky. From her excited eyes to her tiny slipper heels, which were striped with layers of real silver and gold, she was like one of those amazing ships that are carved complete in a bottle. She was finished with that delicacy, with that care; as though the long lifetime of some worker in fragility had been used to make her so. John Chestnut wanted to take her up in his hands, turn her this way and that, examine the tip of a slipper or the tip of an ear or squint closely at the fairy stuff from which her lashes were made.

"Who's that?" She pointed suddenly to a handsome Latin at a table over the way.

"That's Roderigo Minerlino, the movie and face-cream star. Perhaps he'll dance after a while."

Rags became suddenly aware of the sound of violins and drums, but the music seemed to come from far away, seemed to float over the crisp night and on to the floor with the added remoteness of a dream.

"The orchestra's on another roof," explained John. "It's a new idea—Look, the entertainment's beginning."

A negro girl, thin as a reed, emerged suddenly from a masked entrance into a circle of harsh barbaric light, startled the music to a wild minor, and commenced to sing a rhythmic, tragic song. The pipe of her body broke abruptly and she began a slow incessant step, without progress and without hope, like the failure of a savage insufficient dream. She had lost Papa Jack, she cried over and over with a hysterical monotony at once despairing and unreconciled. One by one the loud horns tried to force her from the steady beat of madness but she listened only to the mutter of the drums which were isolating her in some lost place in time, among many thousand forgotten years. After the failure of the piccolo, she made herself again into a thin brown line, wailed once with sharp and terrible intensity, then vanished into sudden darkness.

"If you lived in New York you wouldn't need to be told who she is," said John when the amber light flashed on. "The next fella is Sheik B. Smith, a comedian of the fatuous, garrulous sort——"

He broke off. Just as the lights went down for the second number Rags had given a long sigh, and leaned forward tensely in her chair. Her eyes were rigid like the eyes of a pointer dog, and John saw that they were fixed on a party that had come through a side entrance, and were arranging themselves around a table in the half-darkness.

The table was shielded with palms, and Rags at first made out only three dim forms. Then she distinguished a fourth who seemed to be placed well behind the other three—a pale oval of a face topped with a glimmer of dark-yellow hair.

"Hello!" ejaculated John. "There's his majesty now."

Her breath seemed to die murmurously in her throat. She was dimly aware that the comedian was now standing in a glow of white light on the dancing floor, that he had been talking for some moments, and that there was a constant ripple of laughter in the air. But her eyes remained motionless, enchanted. She saw one of the party bend and whisper to another, and after the low glitter of a match the bright button of a cigarette end gleamed in the background. How long it was before she moved she did not know. Then something seemed to happen to her eyes, something white, something terribly urgent, and she wrenched about sharply to find herself full in the centre of a baby spot-light from above. She became aware that words were being said to her from somewhere, and that a quick trail of laughter was circling the roof, but the light blinded her, and instinctively she made a half-movement from her chair.

"Sit still!" John was whispering across the table. "He picks somebody out for this every night."

Then she realized—it was the comedian, Sheik B. Smith. He was talking to her, arguing with her—about something that seemed incredibly funny to every one else, but came to her ears only as a blur of muddled sound. Instinctively she had composed her face at the first shock of the light and now she smiled. It was a gesture of rare self-possession. Into this smile she insinuated a vast impersonality, as if she were unconscious of the light, unconscious of his attempt to play upon her loveliness—but amused at an infinitely removed *him*, whose darts might have been thrown just as successfully at the moon. She was no longer a "lady"—a lady would have been harsh or pitiful or absurd; Rags stripped her attitude to a sheer consciousness of her own impervious beauty, sat there glittering until the comedian began to feel alone as he had never felt alone before. At a signal from him the spot-light was switched suddenly out. The moment was over.

The moment was over, the comedian left the floor, and the far-away music began. John leaned toward her.

"I'm sorry. There really wasn't anything to do. You were wonderful."

She dismissed the incident with a casual laugh—then she started, there were now only two men sitting at the table across the floor.

"He's gone!" she exclaimed in quick distress.

"Don't worry—he'll be back. He's got to be awfully careful, you see, so he's probably waiting outside with one of his aides until it gets dark again."

"Why has he got to be careful?"

"Because he's not supposed to be in New York. He's even under one of his second-string names."

The lights dimmed again, and almost immediately a tall man appeared out of the darkness and approached their table.

"May I introduce myself?" he said rapidly to John in a supercilious British voice. "Lord Charles Este, of Baron Marchbanks' party." He glanced at John closely as if to be sure that he appreciated the significance of the name.

John nodded.

"That is between ourselves, you understand."

"Of course."

Rags groped on the table for her untouched champagne, and tipped the glassful down her throat.

"Baron Marchbanks requests that your companion will join his party during this number."

Both men looked at Rags. There was a moment's pause.

"Very well," she said, and glanced back again interrogatively at John. Again he nodded. She rose and with her heart beating wildly threaded the tables, making the half-circuit of the room; then melted, a slim figure in shimmering gold, into the table set in half-darkness.

IV

The number drew to a close, and John Chestnut sat alone at his table, stirring auxiliary bubbles in his glass of champagne. Just before the lights went on, there was a soft rasp of gold cloth, and Rags, flushed and breathing quickly, sank into her chair. Her eyes were shining with tears.

John looked at her moodily.

"Well, what did he say?"

"He was very quiet."

"Didn't he say a word?"

Her hand trembled as she took up her glass of champagne.

"He just looked at me while it was dark. And he said a few conventional things. He was like his pictures, only he looks very bored and tired. He didn't even ask my name."

"Is he leaving New York to-night?"

"In half an hour. He and his aides have a car outside, and they expect to be over the border before dawn."

"Did you find him—fascinating?"

She hesitated and then slowly nodded her head.

"That's what everybody says," admitted John glumly. "Do they expect you back there?"

"I don't know." She looked uncertainly across the floor but the celebrated personage had again withdrawn from his table to some retreat outside. As she turned back an utterly strange young man who had been standing for a moment in the main entrance came toward them hurriedly. He was a deathly pale person in a dishevelled and inappropriate business suit, and he had laid a trembling hand on John Chestnut's shoulder.

"Monte!" exclaimed John, starting up so suddenly that he upset his champagne. "What is it? What's the matter?"

"They've picked up the trail!" said the young man in a shaken whisper. He looked around. "I've got to speak to you alone."

John Chestnut jumped to his feet, and Rags noticed that his face too had become white as the napkin in his hand. He excused himself and they retreated to an unoccupied table a few feet away. Rags watched them curiously for a moment, then she resumed her scrutiny of the table across the floor. Would she be asked to come back? The prince had simply risen and bowed and gone outside. Perhaps she should have waited until he returned, but though she was still tense with excitement she had, to some extent, become Rags Martin-Jones again. Her curiosity was satisfied—any new urge must come from him. She wondered if she had really felt an intrinsic charm—she wondered especially if he had in any marked way responded to her beauty.

The pale person called Monte disappeared and John returned to the table. Rags was startled to find that a tremendous change had come over him. He lurched into his chair like a drunken man.

"John! What's the matter?"

Instead of answering, he reached for the champagne bottle, but his fingers were trembling so that the splattered wine made a wet yellow ring around his glass.

"Are you sick?"

"Rags," he said unsteadily, "I'm all through."

"What do you mean?"

"I'm all through, I tell you." He managed a sickly smile. "There's been a warrant out for me for over an hour."

"What have you done?" she demanded in a frightened voice. "What's the warrant for?"

The lights went out for the next number, and he collapsed suddenly over the table.

"What is it?" she insisted, with rising apprehension. She leaned forward—his answer was barely audible.

"Murder?" She could feel her body grow cold as ice.

He nodded. She took hold of both arms and tried to shake him upright, as one shakes a coat into place. His eyes were rolling in his head.

"Is it true? Have they got proof?"

Again he nodded drunkenly.

"Then you've got to get out of the country now! Do you understand, John? You've got to get out *now*, before they come looking for you here!"

He loosed a wild glance of terror toward the entrance.

"Oh, God!" cried Rags, "why don't you do something?" Her eyes strayed here and there in desperation, became suddenly fixed. She drew in her breath sharply, hesitated, and then whispered fiercely into his ear.

"If I arrange it, will you go to Canada to-night?"

"How?"

"I'll arrange it—if you'll pull yourself together a little. This is Rags talking to you, don't you understand, John? I want you to sit here and not move until I come back!"

A minute later she had crossed the room under cover of the darkness.

"Baron Marchbanks," she whispered softly, standing just behind his chair.

He motioned her to sit down.

"Have you room in your car for two more passengers to-night?"

One of the aides turned around abruptly.

"His lordship's car is full," he said shortly.

"It's terribly urgent." Her voice was trembling.

"Well," said the prince hesitantly, "I don't know."

Lord Charles Este looked at the prince and shook his head.

"I don't think it's advisable. This is a ticklish business anyhow with contrary orders from home. You know we agreed there'd be no complications."

The prince frowned.

"This isn't a complication," he objected.

Este turned frankly to Rags.

"Why is it urgent?"

Rags hesitated.

"Why"—she flushed suddenly—"it's a runaway marriage."

The prince laughed.

"Good!" he exclaimed. "That settles it. Este is just being official. Bring him over right away. We're leaving shortly, what?"

Este looked at his watch.

"Right now!"

Rags rushed away. She wanted to move the whole party from the roof while the lights were still down.

"Hurry!" she cried in John's ear. "We're going over the border—with the Prince of Wales. You'll be safe by morning."

He looked up at her with dazed eyes. She hurriedly paid the check, and seizing his arm piloted him as inconspicuously as possible to the other table, where she introduced him with a word. The prince acknowledged his presence by shaking hands— the aides nodded, only faintly concealing their displeasure.

"We'd better start," said Este, looking impatiently at his watch.

They were on their feet when suddenly an exclamation broke from all of them—two policemen and a red-haired man in plain clothes had come in at the main door.

"Out we go," breathed Este, impelling the party toward the side entrance. "There's going to be some kind of riot here." He swore—two more bluecoats barred the exit there. They paused uncertainly. The plain-clothes man was beginning a careful inspection of the people at the tables.

Este looked sharply at Rags and then at John, who shrank back behind the palms.

"Is that one of your revenue fellas out there?" demanded Este.

"No," whispered Rags. "There's going to be trouble. Can't we get out this entrance?"

The prince with rising impatience sat down again in his chair.

"Let me know when you chaps are ready to go." He smiled at Rags. "Now just suppose we all get in trouble just for that jolly face of yours."

Then suddenly the lights went up. The plainclothes man whirled around quickly and sprang to the middle of the cabaret floor.

"Nobody try to leave this room!" he shouted. "Sit down, that party behind the palms! Is John M. Chestnut in this room?"

Rags gave a short involuntary cry.

"Here!" cried the detective to the policeman behind him. "Take a look at that funny bunch across over there. Hands up, you men!"

"My God!" whispered Este, "we've got to get out of here!" He turned to the prince. "This won't do, Ted. You can't be seen here. I'll stall them off while you get down to the car."

He took a step toward the side entrance.

"Hands up, there!" shouted the plain-clothes man. "And when I say hands up I mean it! Which one of you's Chestnut?"

"You're mad!" cried Este. "We're British subjects. We're not involved in this affair in any way!"

A woman screamed somewhere, and there was a general movement toward the elevator, a movement which stopped short before the muzzles of two automatic pistols. A girl next to Rags collapsed in a dead faint to the floor, and at the same moment the music on the other roof began to play.

"Stop that music!" bellowed the plain-clothes man. "And get some earrings on that whole bunch—quick!"

Two policemen advanced toward the party, and simultaneously Este and the other aides drew their revolvers, and, shielding the prince as they best could, began to edge toward the side. A shot rang out and then another, followed by a crash of silver and china as half a dozen diners overturned their tables and dropped quickly behind.

The panic became general. There were three shots in quick succession, and then a fusillade. Rags saw Este firing coolly at the eight amber lights above, and a thick fume of gray smoke began to fill the air. As a strange undertone to the shouting and screaming came the incessant clamor of the distant jazz band.

Then in a moment it was all over. A shrill whistle rang out over the roof, and through the smoke Rags saw John Chestnut advancing toward the plain-clothes man, his hands held out in a gesture of surrender. There was a last nervous cry, a chill clatter as some one inadvertently stepped into a pile of dishes, and then a heavy silence fell on the roof—even the band seemed to have died away.

"It's all over!" John Chestnut's voice rang out wildly on the night air. "The party's over. Everybody who wants to can go home!"

Still there was silence—Rags knew it was the silence of awe— the strain of guilt had driven John Chestnut insane.

"It was a great performance," he was shouting. "I want to thank you one and all. If you can find any tables still standing, champagne will be served as long as you care to stay."

It seemed to Rags that the roof and the high stars suddenly began to swim round and round. She saw John take the detective's hand and shake it heartily, and she watched the detective grin and pocket his gun. The music had recommenced, and the girl who had fainted was suddenly dancing with Lord Charles Este in the corner. John was running here and there patting people on the back, and laughing and shaking hands. Then he was coming toward her, fresh and innocent as a child.

"Wasn't it wonderful?" he cried.

Rags felt a faintness stealing over her. She groped backward with her hand toward a chair.

"What was it?" she cried dazedly. "Am I dreaming?"

"Of course not! You're wide awake. I made it up, Rags, don't you see? I made up the whole thing for you. I had it invented! The only thing real about it was my name!"

She collapsed suddenly against his coat, clung to his lapels, and would have wilted to the floor if he had not caught her quickly in his arms.

"Some champagne—quick!" he called, and then he shouted at the Prince of Wales, who stood near by. "Order my car quick, you! Miss Martin-Jones has fainted from excitement."

V

The skyscraper rose bulkily through thirty tiers of windows before it attenuated itself to a graceful sugar-loaf of shining white. Then it darted up again another hundred feet, thinned to a mere oblong tower in its last fragile aspiration toward the sky. At the highest of its high windows Rags Martin-Jones stood full in the stiff breeze, gazing down at the city.

"Mr. Chestnut wants to know if you'll come right in to his private office."

Obediently her slim feet moved along the carpet into a high, cool chamber overlooking the harbor and the wide sea.

John Chestnut sat at his desk, waiting, and Rags walked to him and put her arms around his shoulder.

189

"Are you sure *you're* real?" she asked anxiously. "Are you absolutely *sure*?"

"You only wrote me a week before you came," he protested modestly, "or I could have arranged a revolution."

"Was the whole thing just *mine*?" she demanded. "Was it a perfectly useless, gorgeous thing, just for me?"

"Useless?" He considered. "Well, it started out to be. At the last minute I invited a big restaurant man to be there, and while you were at the other table I sold him the whole idea of the night-club."

He looked at his watch.

"I've got one more thing to do—and then we've got just time to be married before lunch." He picked up his telephone. "Jackson? . . . Send a triplicated cable to Paris, Berlin, and Budapest and have those two bogus dukes who tossed up for Schwartzberg-Rhineminster chased over the Polish border. If the Dutchy won't act, lower the rate of exchange to point triple zero naught two. Also, that idiot Blutchdak is in the Balkans again, trying to start a new war. Put him on the first boat for New York or else throw him in a Greek jail."

He rang off, turned to the startled cosmopolite with a laugh.

"The next stop is the City Hall. Then, if you like, we'll run over to Paris."

"John," she asked him intently, "who was the Prince of Wales?"

He waited till they were in the elevator, dropping twenty floors at a swoop. Then he leaned forward and tapped the lift-boy on the shoulder.

"Not so fast, Cedric. This lady isn't used to falls from high places."

The elevator-boy turned around, smiled. His face was pale, oval, framed in yellow hair. Rags blushed like fire.

"Cedric's from Wessex," explained John. "The resemblance is, to say the least, amazing. Princes are not particularly discreet, and I suspect Cedric of being a Guelph in some left-handed way."

Rags took the monocle from around her neck and threw the

ribbon over Cedric's head.

"Thank you," she said simply, "for the second greatest thrill of my life."

John Chestnut began rubbing his hands together in a commercial gesture.

"Patronize this place, lady," he besought her. "Best bazaar in the city!"

"What have you got for sale?"

"Well, m'selle, to-day we have some perfectly bee-*oo*-tiful love."

"Wrap it up, Mr. Merchant," cried Rags Martin-Jones. "It looks like a bargain to me."

THE DANCE

First published in
The Red Book Magazine, June, 1926

All my life I have had a rather curious horror of small towns: not suburbs; they are quite a different matter — but the little lost cities of New Hampshire and Georgia and Kansas, and upper New York. I was born in New York City, and even as a little girl I never had any fear of the streets or the strange foreign faces — but on the occasions when I've been in the sort of place I'm referring to, I've been oppressed with the consciousness that there was a whole hidden life, a whole series of secret implications, significances and terrors, just below the surface, of which I knew nothing. In the cities everything good or bad eventually comes out, comes out of people's hearts, I mean. Life moves about, moves on, vanishes. In the small towns — those between 5,000 and 25,000 people — old hatreds, old and unforgotten affairs, ghostly scandals and tragedies, seem unable to die, but live on all tangled up with the ebb and flow of outward life.

Nowhere has this sensation come over me more insistently than in the south. Once out of Atlanta and Birmingham and New Orleans, I often have the feeling that I can no longer communicate with the people around me. The men and the girls speak a language wherein courtesy is combined with violence, fanatic morality with corn-drinking recklessness, in a fashion which I can't understand. In *Huckleberry Finn* Mark Twain described some of those towns perched along the Mississippi River, with their fierce feuds and their equally fierce revivals —

and some of them haven't fundamentally changed beneath their new surface of flibbers and radios. They are deeply uncivilized to this day.

I speak of the South because it was in a small southern city of this type that I once saw the surface crack for a minute and something savage, uncanny and frightening rear its head. Then the surface closed again — and when I have gone back there since, I've been surprised to find myself as charmed as ever by the magnolia trees and the singing darkies in the street and the sensuous warm nights. I have been charmed, too, by the bountiful hospitality and the languorous easy-going outdoor life and the almost universal good manners. But all too frequently I am the prey of a vivid nightmare that recalls what I experienced in that town five years ago.

Davis — that is not its real name — has a population of about 20,000 people, one-third of them coloured. It is a cotton-mill town, and the workers of that trade, several thousand and gaunt and ignorant 'poor whites', live together in an ill-reputed section known as 'Cotton Hollow'. The population of Davis has varied in its seventy-five years. Once it was under consideration for the capital of the State, and so the older families and their kin form a little aristocracy, even when individually they have sunk to destitution.

That winter I'd made the usual round in New York until about April, when I decided I never wanted to see another invitation again. I was tired and I wanted to go to Europe for a rest; but the baby panic of 1921 hit father's business, and so it was suggested that I go South and visit Aunt Musidora Hale instead.

Vaguely I imagined that I was going to the country, but on the day I arrived the *Davis Courier* published a hilarious old picture of me on its society page, and I found I was in for another season. On a small scale, of course: there were Saturday-night dances at the little country-club with its nine-hole golf-course, and some informal dinner parties and several attractive and attentive boys. I didn't have a dull time at all, and when after three weeks I wanted to go home, it wasn't because I was bored. On the contrary I wanted to go home because I'd allowed myself to get rather interested in a young man named Charley Kincaid, without realizing that he was engaged to another girl.

We'd been drawn together from the first because he was almost the only boy in town who'd gone North to college, and I was still young enough to think that America revolved around Harvard and Princeton and Yale. He liked me too — I could see that; but when I heard that his engagement to a girl named Marie Bannerman had been announced six months before, there was nothing for me except to go away. The town was too small to avoid people, and though so far there hadn't been any talk, I was sure that — well, that if we kept meeting, the emotion we were beginning to feel would somehow get into words. I'm not mean enough to take a man away from another girl.

Marie Bannerman was almost a beauty. Perhaps she would have been a beauty if she'd had any clothes, and if she hadn't used bright pink rouge in two high spots on her cheeks and powdered her nose and chin to a funereal white. Her hair was shining black; her features were lovely; and an affection of one eye kept it always half-closed and gave an air of humourous mischief to her face.

I was leaving on a Monday, and on Saturday night a crowd of us dined at the country-club as usual before the dance. There was Joe Cable, the son of a former governor, a handsome dissipated and yet somehow charming young man; Catherine Jones, a pretty, sharp-eyed girl with an exquisite figure, who under her rouge might have been any age from eighteen to twenty-five; Marie Bannerman; Charley Kincaid; myself and two or three others.

I loved to listen to the genial flow of bizarre neighbourhood anecdote at this kind of party. For instance, one of the girls, together with her entire family, had that afternoon been evicted from her house for non-payment of rent. She told the story wholly without self-consciousness, merely as something troublesome but amusing. And I loved the banter which presumed every girl to be infinitely beautiful and attractive, and every man to have been secretly and hopelessly in love with every girl present from their respective cradles.

'We liked to die laughin'' . . . '— said he was fixin' to shoot him without he stayed away.' The girls 'clared to heaven'; the men 'took oath' on inconsequential statements. 'How come you nearly about forgot to come by for me —' and the incessant Honey, Honey, Honey, Honey, until the word seemed to roll like a genial liquid from heart to heart.

Outside, the May night was hot, a still night, velvet, soft-pawed, splattered thick with stars. It drifted heavy and sweet into the large room where we sat and where we would later dance, with no sound in it except the occasional long crunch of an arriving car on the drive. Just at that moment I hated to leave Davis as I never had hated to leave a town before — I felt that I wanted to spend my life in this town, drifting and dancing forever through these long, hot, romantic nights.

Yet horror was already hanging over that little party, was waiting tensely among us, an uninvited guest, and telling off the hours until it could show its pale and blinding face. Beneath the chatter and laughter something was going on, something secret and obscure that I didn't know.

Presently the coloured orchestra arrived, followed by the first trickle of the dance crowd. An enormous red-faced man in muddy knee boots and with a revolver strapped around his waist, clumped in and paused for a moment at our table before going upstairs to the locker-room. It was Bill Abercrombie, the sheriff, the son of Congressman Abercrombie. Some of the boys asked him half-whispered questions, and he replied in an attempt at an undertone.

'Yes . . . He's in the swamp all right; farmer saw him near the crossroads store . . . Like to have a shot at him myself.'

I asked the boy next to me what was the matter.

'Nigger case,' he said, 'over in Kisco, about two miles from here. He's hiding in the swamp, and they're going in after him tomorrow.'

'What'll they do to him?'

'Hang him, I guess.'

The notion of the forlorn darky crouching dismally in a desolate bog waiting for dawn and death depressed me for a moment. Then the feeling passed and was forgotten.

After dinner Charley Kincaid and I walked out on the veranda — he had just heard that I was going away. I kept as close to the others as I could, answering his words but not his eyes — something inside me was protesting against leaving him on such a casual note. The temptation was strong to let something flicker up between us here at the end. I wanted him to kiss me — my heart promised that if he kissed me, just once, it would accept with equanimity the idea of never seeing him any more; but my mind knew it wasn't so.

The other girls began to drift inside and upstairs to the dressing-room to improve their complexions, and with Charley still beside me, I followed. Just at that moment I wanted to cry — perhaps my eyes were already blurred, or perhaps it was my haste lest they should be, but I opened the door of a small card-room by mistake and with my error the tragic machinery of the night began to function. In the card-room, not five feet from us, stood Marie Bannerman, Charley's fiancée, and Joe Cable. They were in each other's arms, absorbed in a passionate and oblivious kiss.

I closed the door quickly and without glancing at Charley opened the right door and ran upstairs.

A few minutes later Marie Bannerman entered the crowded dressing-room. She saw me and came over, smiling in a sort of mock despair, but she breathed quickly, and the smile trembled a little on her mouth.

'You won't say a word, honey, will you?' she whispered.

'Of course not.' I wondered how that could matter, now that

Charley Kincaid knew.

'Who else was it that saw us?'

'Only Charley Kincaid and I.'

'Oh!' She looked a little puzzled; then she added: 'He didn't wait to say anything, honey. When we came out he was just going out the door. I thought he was going to wait and romp all over Joe.'

'How about his romping all over you?' I couldn't help asking.

'Oh, he'll do that.' She laughed wryly. 'But, honey, I know how to handle him. It's just when he's first mad that I'm scared of him — he's got an awful temper.' She whistled reminiscently. 'I know, because this happened once before.'

I wanted to slap her. Turning my back, I walked away on the pretext of borrowing a pin from Katie, the Negro maid. Catherine Jones was claiming the latter's attention with a short gingham garment which needed repair.

'What's that?' I asked.

'Dancing-dress,' she answered shortly, her mouth full of pins. When she took them out, she added: 'It's all come to pieces — I've used it so much.'

'Are you going to dance here tonight?'

'Going to try.'

Somebody had told me that she wanted to be a dancer — that she had taken lessons in New York.

'Can I help you fix anything?'

'No, thanks — unless — can you sew? Katie gets so excited Saturday night that she's no good for anything except fetching pins. I'd be everlasting grateful to you, honey.'

I had reasons for not wanting to go downstairs just yet, and so I sat down and worked on her dress for half an hour. I wondered if Charley had gone home, if I would ever see him again — I scarcely dared to wonder if what he had seen would set him free, ethically. When I went down finally he was not in sight.

The room was now crowded; the tables had been removed and dancing was general. At that time, just after the war, all Southern boys had a way of agitating their heels from side to side, pivoting on the ball of the foot as they danced, and to acquiring this accomplishment I had devoted many hours. There were plenty of stags, almost all of them cheerful with corn-liquor; I refused on an average at least two drinks a dance. Even when it is mixed with a soft drink, as is the custom, rather than gulped from the neck of a warm bottle, it is a formidable proposition. Only a few girls like Catherine Jones took an occasional sip from some boy's flask down at the dark end of the veranda.

I liked Catherine Jones — she seemed to have more energy than these other girls, though Aunt Musidora sniffed rather contemptuously whenever Catherine stopped for me in her car to go to the movies, remarking that she guessed 'the bottom rail had gotten to be the top rail now'. Her family were 'new and common', but it seemed to be that perhaps her very commonness was an asset. Almost every girl in Davis confided in me at one time or another that her ambition was to 'get away to New York', but only Catherine Jones had actually taken the step of studying stage dancing with that end in view.

She was often asked to dance at these Saturday night affairs, something 'classic' or perhaps an acrobatic clog — on one memorable occasion she had annoyed the governing board by a 'shimee' (then the scapegrace of jazz), and the novel and somewhat startling excuse made for her was that she was 'so tight she didn't know what she was doing, anyhow'. She impressed me as a curious girl, arid I was eager to see what she would produce tonight.

At twelve o'clock the music always ceased, as dancing was forbidden on Sunday morning. So at 11.30 a vast fanfaronade of drum and cornet beckoned the dancers and the couples on the verandas, and the ones in the cars outside, and the stragglers from the bar, into the ballroom. Chairs were brought in and galloped up *en masse* and with a great racket to the slightly raised platform. The orchestra had evacuated this and taken a place beside. Then, as the rearward lights were lowered, they began to play a tune accompanied by a curious drumbeat that I had never heard before, and simultaneously Catherine Jones appeared upon the platform. She wore the short, country girl's dress upon which I had lately laboured, and a wide sun bonnet under which her face, stained yellow with powder, looked out at us with rolling eyes and a vacant negroid leer. She began to dance.

I had never seen anything like it before, and until five years later, I wasn't to see it again. It was the Charleston — it must have been the Charleston. I remember the double drum-beat like a shouted 'Hey! Hey!' and the swing of the arms and the odd knock-kneed effect. She had picked it up, heaven knows where.

Her audience, familiar with Negro rhythms, leaned forward eagerly — even to them it was something new, but it is stamped on my mind as clearly and indelibly as though I had seen it yesterday. The figure on the platform swinging and stamping, the excited orchestra, the waiters grinning in the doorway of the bar, and all around, through many windows, the soft languorous Southern night seeping in from swamp and cottonfield and lush foliage and brown, warm streams. At what point a feeling of tense uneasiness began to steal over me I don't know. The dance could scarcely have taken ten minutes; perhaps the first beats of the barbaric music disquieted me — long before it was over, I was sitting rigid in my seat, and my eyes were wandering here and there around the hall, passing along the rows of shadowy faces as if seeking some security that was no longer there.

I'm not a nervous type; nor am I given to panic; but for a moment I was afraid that if the music and the dance didn't stop, I'd be hysterical. Something was happening all about me. I knew it as well as if I could see into these unknown souls. Things were happening, but one thing especially was leaning over so close that it almost touched us, that it did touch us . . . I almost screamed as a hand brushed accidentally against my back.

The music stopped. There was applause and protracted cries of encore, but Catherine Jones shook her head definitely at the orchestra leader and made as though to leave the platform. The appeals for more continued — again she shook her head, and it seemed to me that her expression was rather angry. Then a strange incident occurred. At the protracted pleading of someone in the front row, the coloured orchestra leader began the vamp of the tune, as if to lure Catherine Jones into changing her mind. Instead she turned toward him, snapped out: 'Didn't you hear me say no?' and then, surprisingly, slapped his face. The music stopped, and an amused murmur terminated abruptly as a muffled but clearly audible shot rang out.

Immediately we were on our feet, for the sound indicated that it had been fired within or near the house. One of the chaperons gave a little scream, but when some wag called out: 'Caesar's in that henhouse again', the momentary alarm dissolved into laughter. The club manager, followed by several curious couples, went out to have a look about, but the rest were already moving around the floor to the strains of 'Good Night, Ladies', which traditionally ended the dance.

I was glad it was over. The man with whom I had come went to get his car, and calling a waiter, I sent him for my golf-clubs, which were upstairs. I strolled out on the porch and waited, wondering again if Charley Kincaid had gone home.

Suddenly I was aware, in that curious way in which you become aware of something that has been going on for several minutes, that there was a tumult inside. Women were shrieking; there was a cry of 'Oh, my God!', then the sounds of a stampede on the inside stairs, and footsteps running back and forth across the ballroom. A girl appeared from somewhere and pitched forward in a dead faint — almost immediately another girl did the same, and I heard a frantic male voice shouting into a telephone. Then, hatless and pale, a young man rushed out on the porch, and with hands that were cold as ice, seized my arm.

'What is it?' I cried. 'A fire? What's happened?'

'Marie Bannerman's dead upstairs in the women's dressing-room. Shot through the throat!'

The rest of that night is a series of visions that seem to have no connection with one another, that follow each other with the sharp instantaneous transitions of scenes in the movies. There was a group who stood arguing on the porch, in voices now raised, now hushed, about what should be done and how every waiter in the club, 'even old Moses', ought to be given the third degree tonight. That a 'nigger' had shot and killed Marie Bannerman was the instant and unquestioned assumption — in the first unreasoning instant, anyone who doubted it would have been under suspicion. The guilty one was said to be Katie Golstein, the coloured maid, who had discovered the body and fainted. It was said to be 'that nigger they were looking for at Kisco.' It was any darky at all.

Within half an hour people began to drift out, each with his little contribution of new discoveries. The crime had been committed with Sheriff Abercrombie's gun — he had hung it, belt and all, in full view on the wall before coming down to dance. It was missing — they were hunting for it now. Instantly killed, the doctor said — bullet had been fired from only a few feet away.

Then a few minutes later another young man came out and made the announcement in a loud, grave voice: 'They've arrested Charley Kincaid.'

My head reeled. Upon the group gathered on the veranda fell an awed, stricken silence.

'Arrested Charley Kincaid!'

'Charley *Kincaid?*'

Why, he was one of the best, one of themselves.

'That's the craziest thing I ever heard of!'

The young man nodded, shocked like the rest, but self-important with his information.

'He wasn't downstairs, when Catherine Jones was dancing —

he says he was in the men's locker-room. And Marie Bannerman told a lot of girls that they'd had a row, and she was scared of what he'd do.'

Again an awed silence.

'That's the craziest thing I ever heard!' someone said again.

'Charley *Kincaid*!'

The narrator waited a moment. Then he added:

'He caught her kissing Joe Cable —'

I couldn't keep silence a minute longer.

'What about it?' I cried out. 'I was with him at the time. He wasn't — he wasn't angry at all.'

They looked at me, their faces startled, confused, unhappy. Suddenly the footsteps of several men sounded loud through the ballroom, and a moment later Charley Kincaid, his face dead white, came out the front door between the Sheriff and another man. Crossing the porch quickly, they descended the steps and disappeared in the darkness. A moment later there was the sound of a starting car.

When an instant later far away down the road I heard the eerie scream of an ambulance, I got up desperately and called to my escort, who formed part of the whispering group.

'I've got to go,' I said. 'I can't stand this. Either take me home or I'll find a place in another car.' Reluctantly he shouldered my clubs — the sight of them made me realize that I now couldn't leave on Monday after all — and followed me down the steps just as the black ambulance curved in at the gate — a ghastly shadow on the bright, starry night.

The situation after the first wild surmises, the first burst of unreasoning loyalty to Charley Kincaid, had died away, was outlined by the *Davis Courier* and by most of the State newspapers in this fashion: Marie Bannerman died in the women's dressing-room of the Davis Country Club from the effects of a shot fired at close quarters from a revolver just after 11.45 o'clock on Saturday night. Many persons had heard the shot; moreover, it had undoubtedly been fired from the revolver of Sheriff Abercrombie, which had been hanging in full sight on the wall of the next room. Abercrombie himself was in the ballroom when the murder took place, as many witnesses could testify. The revolver was not found.

So far as was known, the only man who had been upstairs at the time the shot was fired was Charley Kincaid. He was engaged to Miss Bannerman, but according to several witnesses they had quarrelled seriously that evening. Miss Bannerman herself had mentioned the quarrel, adding that she was afraid and wanted to keep away from him until he cooled off.

Charles Kincaid asserted that at the time the shot was fired he was in the men's locker-room — where, indeed, he was found, immediately after the discovery of Miss Bannerman's body. He denied having had any words with Miss Bannerman at all. He had heard the shot but if he thought anything of it, he thought that 'someone was potting cats out-doors.'

Why had he chosen to remain in the locker-room during the dance?

No reason at all. He was tired. He was waiting until Miss Bannerman wanted to go home.

The body was discovered by Katie Golstein, the coloured maid, who herself was found in a faint when the crowd of girls surged upstairs for their coats. Returning from the kitchen, where she had been getting a bite to eat, Katie had found Miss Bannerman, her dress wet with blood, already dead on the floor.

Both the police and the newspapers attached importance to the geography of the country-club's second storey. It consisted of a row of three rooms — the women's dressing-room and the men's locker-room at either end, and in the middle a room which was used as a cloak-room and for the storage of golf-clubs. The women's and men's rooms had no outlet except into this chamber, which was connected by one stairs with the ball-room below, and by another with the kitchen. According to the testimony of three Negro cooks and the white caddy-master, no one but Katie Golstein had gone up the kitchen stairs that night.

As I remember it after five years, the foregoing is a pretty accurate summary of the situation when Charley Kincaid was accused of first-degree murder and committed for trial. Other people, chiefly Negroes, were suspected (at the loyal instigation of Charley Kincaid's friends), and several arrests were made, but nothing ever came of them, and upon what grounds they were based I have long forgotten. One group, in spite of the disappearance of the pistol, claimed persistently that it was a suicide and suggested some ingenious reasons to account for the absence of the weapon.

Now when it is known Marie Bannerman happened to die so savagely and so violently, it would be easy for me, of all people, to say that I believed in Charley Kincaid all the time. But I didn't. I thought that he had killed her, and at the same time I knew that I loved him with all my heart. That it was I who first happened upon the evidence which set him free was due not to any faith in his innocence but to a strange vividness with which, in moods of excitement, certain scenes stamp themselves on my memory, so that I can remember every detail and how that detail struck me at the time.

It was one afternoon early in July, when the case against Charley Kincaid seemed to be at its strongest, that the horror of the actual murder slipped away from me for a moment and I began to think about other incidents of that same haunted night. Something Marie Bannerman had said to me in the dressing-room persistently eluded me, bothered me — not because I believed it to be important, but simply because I couldn't remember. It was gone from me, as if it had been a part of the fantastic undercurrent of small-town life which I had felt so strongly that evening, the sense that things were in the air, old secrets, old loves and feuds, and unresolved situations, that I could never fully understand. Just for a minute it seemed to me that Marie Bannerman had pushed aside the curtain; then it had dropped into place again — the house into which I might have looked was dark now forever.

Another incident, perhaps less important, also haunted me. The tragic events of a few minutes after had driven it from everyone's mind, but I had a strong impression that for a brief space of time I wasn't the only one to be surprised. When the audience had demanded an encore from Catherine Jones, her unwillingness to dance again had been so acute that she had been driven to the point of slapping the orchestra leader's face. The discrepancy between his offence and the venom of the rebuff recurred to me again and again. It wasn't natural — or, more important, it hadn't seemed natural. In view of the fact that Catherine Jones had been drinking, it was explicable, but it worried me now as it had worried me then. Rather to lay its ghost than to do any investigating, I pressed an obliging young man into service and called on the leader of the band.

His name was Thomas, a very dark, very simple-hearted virtuoso of the traps, and it took less than ten minutes to find out that Catherine Jones' gesture had surprised him as much as it had me. He had known her a long time, seen her at dances since she was a little girl — why, the very dance she did that night was one she had rehearsed with his orchestra a week before. And a few days later she had come to him and said she was sorry.

'I knew she would,' he concluded. 'She's a right good-hearted girl. My sister Katie was her nurse from when she was born up to the time she went to school.'

'Your sister?'

'Katie. She's the maid out at the country-club. Katie Golstein. You been reading 'bout her in the papers in 'at Charley Kincaid case. She's the maid. Katie Golstein. She's the maid at the country-club what found the body of Miss Bannerman.'

'So Katie was Miss Catherine Jones' nurse?'

'Yes ma'am.'

Going home, stimulated but unsatisfied, I asked my companion a quick question.

'Were Catherine and Marie good friends?'

'Oh, yes,' he answered without hesitation. 'All the girls are good friends here, except when two of them are tryin' to get hold of the same man. Then they warm each other up a little.'

'Why do you suppose Catherine hasn't married? Hasn't she got lots of beaux?'

'Off and on. She only likes people for a day or so at a time. That is — all except Joe Cable.'

Now a scene burst upon me, broke over me like a dissolving wave. And suddenly, my mind shivering from the impact, I remembered what Marie Bannerman had said to me in the dressing-room: 'Who else was it that saw?' She had caught a glimpse of someone else, a figure passing so quickly that she could not identify it, out of the corner of her eye.

And suddenly I seemed to see that figure, as if I too had been vaguely conscious of it at the time, just as one is aware of a familiar gait or outline on the street long before there is any flicker of recognition. On the corner of my own eye was stamped a hurrying figure — that might have been Catherine Jones.

But when the shot was fired, Catherine Jones was in full view of over fifty people. Was it credible that Katie Golstein, a woman of fifty, who as a nurse had been known and trusted by three generations of Davis people, would shoot down a young girl in cold blood at Catherine Jones' command?

'*But when the shot was fired, Catherine Jones was in full view of over fifty people.*'

That sentence beat in my head all night, taking on fantastic variations, dividing itself into phrases, segments, individual words.

'*But when the shot was fired* — Catherine Jones was in full view — of over fifty people.'

When the shot was fired! What shot? The shot we heard. When the shot was fired . . . When the shot was fired . . .

The next morning at nine o'clock, with the pallor of sleeplessness buried under a quantity of paint such as I had never worn before or have since, I walked up a rickety flight of stairs to the Sheriff's office.

Abercrombie, engrossed in his morning's mail, looked up curiously as I came in the door.

'Catherine Jones did it,' I cried, struggling to keep the hysteria out of my voice. 'She killed Marie Bannerman with a shot we didn't hear because the orchestra was playing and everybody was pushing up the chairs. The shot we heard was when Katie fired the pistol out of the window after the music was stopped. To give Catherine an alibi!'

I was right — as everyone now knows, but for a week, until Katie Golstein broke down under a fierce and ruthless inquisition, nobody believed me. Even Charley Kincaid, as he afterward confessed, didn't dare to think it could be true.

What had been the relations between Catherine and Joe Cable no one ever knew, but evidently she had determined that his clandestine affair with Marie Bannerman had gone too far.

Then Marie chanced to come into the women's room while Catherine was dressing for her dance — and there again there is a certain obscurity, for Catherine always claimed that Marie got the revolver, threatened her with it and that in the ensuing struggle the trigger was pulled. In spite of everything, I always rather liked Catherine Jones, but in justice it must be said that only a simple-minded and very exceptional jury would have let her off with five years.

And in just about five years from her commitment my husband and I are going to make a round of the New York musical shows and look hard at all the members of the chorus from the very front row.

After the shooting she must have thought quickly. Katie was told to wait until the music stopped, fire the revolver out of the window and then hide it — Catherine Jones neglected to specify where. Katie, on the verge of collapse, obeyed instructions, but she was never able to specify where she had hid the revolver. And no one ever knew until a year later, when Charley and I were on our honeymoon and Sheriff Abercrombie's ugly weapon dropped out of my golf-bag on to a Hot Springs golf-links. The bag must have been standing just outside the dressing-room door; Katie's trembling hand had dropped the revolver into the first aperture she could see.

We live in New York. Small towns make us both uncomfortable. Every day we read about the crimewaves in the big cities, but at least a wave is something tangible that you can provide against. What I dread above all things is the unknown depths, the incalculable ebb and flow, the secret shapes of things that drift through opaque darkness under the surface of the sea.

www.ingramcontent.com/pod-product-compliance
Lightning Source LLC
Chambersburg PA
CBHW021657110726
47902CB00007B/1962